EMERALD

Recent Titles by Iris Gower

THE CORDWAINERS SERIES

OYSTER CATCHERS
HONEY'S FARM
ARIAN
SEA MISTRESS
THE WILD SEED

FIREBIRD

EMERALD

Iris Gower

This title first published in Great Britain 1998 by
SEVERN HOUSE PUBLISHERS LTD of
9–15 High Street, Sutton, Surrey SM1 1DF.
Originally published 1973 in the USA under the title
The Green Cape and pseudonym *Susanne Richardson*.
This title first published in the USA 1998 by
SEVERN HOUSE PUBLISHERS INC., of
595 Madison Avenue, New York, NY 10022.

British Library Cataloguing in Publication Data

Gower,   Iris
        Emerald
        1.   Swansea (Wales) - Fiction
        2.   Romantic suspense novels
        1. Title
        823.9'14 [F]

        ISBN 0-7278-5361-9

Typeset by Palimpsest Book Production Ltd,
Polmont, Stirlingshire, Scotland.
Printed and bound in Great Britain by
MPG Books Ltd, Bodmin, Cornwall.

CHAPTER ONE

Candlelight flickered like ghostly fingers on the polished wood of the table and threw frenzied images against the heavily curtained windows.

I suppose it was proper that the evening sun should be excluded from a house of mourning, and yet my aunt had loved the windows thrown wide to embrace the last of the summer warmth.

I sat on the very edge of my chair, nervously crumpling the lace of my handkerchief into a ball and acutely aware of the two tall strangers who were discussing my future in low, discreet voices.

From under reddened lids I studied them both, miserably certain that, as an unmarried kinswoman, I would be a responsibility and probably not in the least welcome.

"Well, my dear, we've come to a decision." The silver-haired gentleman, who was apparently my uncle, though we'd never even seen each other until now, sat at my side, a sympathetic smile on his face. A lump came to my throat that was partly caused by fear but mostly by emotion at the unexpected kindness in his voice.

"Greyson will be staying on here, at least for the time being."

He smiled reassuringly, waving a hand toward the thin, dark young man who remained standing before the large fireplace as if declaring that he was already the master of Winston.

"Aunt Grace made him her heir. It was her wish that he run the estate as he sees fit."

He patted my hand, and I felt a sudden urge to scream out, "What's to become of me?" With an effort I managed to regain my control and waited for him to continue.

"I know how you must feel—this has always been your home—but you will be happy with me. I've a lovely home in Wales. You'll grow to love it there, I'm sure."

The colors in the pattern of the carpet merged into a haze before my eyes. So I was to leave my home, the place that held all the memories of my childhood within its mellowed walls. I looked up in sudden antagonism at my cousin, who stood aloof, not comprehending the anguish inside me.

"Why can't I stay here?" The words burst from me in a voice I hardly recognized. "I assure you, cousin, I will not intrude upon you in any way at all."

"Come, come, Charlotte, it would not be correct.

You must surely see that. After all, you are a child no longer."

Greyson looked down at me, his eyes so dark I could read no expression in them. But his implication was obvious. I was almost twenty-one, and in his eyes, an old maid.

I felt the color rise to my cheeks and bit my lip to stop the hot tears from spilling over. On no account would I show him how cruelly his words had stung. I turned to the older man.

"I have no means of my own, then? Didn't Aunt Grace leave me anything?"

As soon as the words were spoken, I realized how cold and calculating they must sound. She had hardly been decently buried, and here I was demanding a share of her worldly goods. Only I knew the real meaning behind the question. I wanted freedom, independence even, from the kindness of my uncle.

He seemed to understand. "Don't you worry your pretty head about any of it, my dear. In a few days we'll go to Wales, and you will have a change of scenery to take your mind off things here."

I sighed and went over to the window, moving the drapes a little and drinking in the beauty of the fields rolling away so peacefully, purpled now by the swiftly falling twilight.

"I think I'll go up to bed, if you'll excuse me." I could hardly bring the words out, but Uncle nodded his approval.

"That's a good idea. This has been a very trying
time for you, but believe me, things will look much
better when you've had a good rest."

He came with me to the door and opened it for
me, stopping me for a moment, his hand on my arm.

"I'll look after you, Charlotte. I want you to be
happy with me, and who knows, in Wales you might
meet some charming young man who'll sweep you off
your feet." He smiled warmly. "You may even end
up marrying Greyson. That would solve your prob-
lems, wouldn't it?"

Somehow I made a polite reply, but the thought of
marrying my cousin made me grit my teeth in anger.

"Jess!" I called more loudly than I'd intended,
and she appeared on the landing, a startled look in
her eyes.

"Yes, miss, is anything wrong?" Her round face
was filled with compassion, and again, in spite of
my anger, tears filled my eyes. Impatiently I dashed
them away.

"I wondered if you could bring me a hot drink,"
I said more quietly. "I've decided to have an early
night."

"You go on in, miss." Jess suffered from a thwarted
maternal instinct. She was not much older than I,
but she insisted upon treating me like a child to be
cosseted. "I'll bring you something that will soothe

you nicely and help you to get off to sleep."

Alone in my room, I sank down disconsolately on the bed, missing Aunt Grace so badly it was like a physical pain. She had been a mother to me and a very dear friend, and it wasn't until I'd seen her eyes closed in death that I'd realized how old she was. Her sparkling eyes and crisp clear wit had given her such an air of eternal youth that I had never even considered a time when I would be without her.

"Here, miss, let's get you tucked into bed." Jess, crackling in her starched apron, put a steaming cup on the bedside table. "You're looking pale, too pale for my liking. Come on; off with your shoes."

Gratefully I submitted to her ministrations. Maybe everything would look better in the morning, though how that could be was a mystery to me. My aunt was dead, and my home now belonged to an arrogant stranger. Sometime in the next few days, I would be taken from everything I loved to go and live in surroundings as foreign to me as unchartered seas.

I put my head down on the pillow and wept.

Summer seemed to fade quickly into a dismal autumn, as if my own misery had somehow affected the weather. Uncle Tom had just about finished his business at Winston, and preparations were in full swing for the movement of my belongings down to the house in Wales. It was decided that Jess would come with me, for that I was profoundly grateful, though I don't think she relished the idea over-much.

My cousin had kept well out of my way, though I would sometimes catch a glimpse of his tall frame as he strode briskly to the stables before breakfast. Resentment grew in me, along with the thought that if I'd been born a male, Winston would now belong to me.

Strangely enough, it was when I was watching Greyson leading out one of the large stallions and almost wishing that I could accompany him for the sheer exhilaration of the ride that I saw Edmund Turner wheel his horse around and gallop off from the estate as if he were in a fine fury. His yellow hair shone even through the dullness of the morning drizzle, lifting in the breeze as he pounded away through the large gates.

Rather hurt at his neglect of me, I hurried downstairs to question my uncle about the visit. Edmund and I had grown up together, and I'd been the first one to congratulate him when he had made such a success of his law studies. In fact, I'd secretly believed it was only his prolonged studies that had prevented him from asking me to marry him up until now.

"Jess, was that Mr. Edmund?" I asked, catching her as she was bringing down yet another of my boxes.

She nodded and fumbled in her pocket. "He asked me to give you this, miss. In a temper he was, because he wasn't allowed to see you himself."

I took the envelope and put it inside my bodice. I would open it later, when I was alone.

"What do you mean, Jess? Why wasn't he allowed to see me?"

Before she could answer, Uncle Tom appeared in the doorway, his face concerned as he took my arm.

"Charlotte, that young man was acting in a very excitable way. I didn't think it wise to allow him to see you just now. I don't want you upset at this time."

I was bewildered. "But Uncle, he's one of my closest friends. I've known Edmund for years. Aunt Grace approved of him, I assure you." Anger flickered through me. "In any case, I'd like the opportunity to make up my own mind about the people I wish to see!"

Uncle Tom frowned, his round face almost babyish in its consternation.

"I'm sorry, Charlotte; I meant well. I was only thinking of you, but it seems I've done the wrong thing." He smiled suddenly. "You are so like your father, did you know that?" His hand fondled my hair. "Those red curls, and a temper to match! He was just the same." He grimaced wryly. "I never did understand him, either!"

Suddenly my anger melted. Uncle Tom couldn't know about Edmund being a special friend; it was I who was being unreasonable.

"Come on, Uncle, let's have breakfast. Perhaps I'll be in a better humor then."

I linked my arm with his, and he flushed with pleasure so that I felt even more ashamed of my outburst.

"Don't worry, Uncle," I said reassuringly. "Edmund will be back, there's no doubt about that. He can be very persistent."

Uncle Tom smiled and patted my hand.

"I'm not surprised at that. My niece *is* a very attractive lady, after all."

He chuckled, and my heart warmed to him. For the first time since Aunt Grace's death, I felt a lightening of my spirits.

Edmund's note was very cryptic. "Come to my office; I must see you!" His untidy signature was scrawled underneath.

"Uncle Tom, I'm thinking of going out today." I strode into the drawing room, not expecting to see my cousin sitting at the writing desk.

"Sorry; he's not here." Greyson lifted his eyebrows in amusement. "It seems you both had the same idea. What a pity you didn't decide earlier; then you could have gone together. As it is, I'm far too busy to come with you. I'm afraid you'll have to go another time."

I stared at him, trying hard to appear icy when inside I was seething with fury.

"I am quite capable of riding a horse alone, cousin," I said, and looked at him defiantly.

Deliberately he put down his pen and, to my discomfort, stood up, towering over me.

"Charlotte, have you no sense of what is fitting, paticularly in these circumstances? How would it look, a young woman so recently bereaved riding around the countryside alone?"

He was quite right, of course. I strode over to the windows and stared out at the soft rain that hung like a mist over the green of the lawns. Suddenly I turned and smiled warmly at him.

"Well, then, Greyson, I'm sure you could put off your letter writing for an hour or two, couldn't you?"

"Charlotte, I had no idea you could be so charming."

He took my reluctant fingers in his large hand and smiled down at me. I found myself staring into his dark eyes, trying to read something of his thoughts. He raised my hand to his lips in a charming gesture, and then, still with a smile on his face, refused to help me.

"I'm very sorry to say no, but as I've told you, I'm far too busy to take a trip into town."

Anger grew and blossomed like a flower in the sun, so that for one moment I almost slapped him. Instead, I jerked my hand away.

"I am never going to ask your help again!" I said coldly, and he made a mock bow.

"I'm not sure if that is meant as a threat or a promise!" He smiled and returned to sit at the desk, taking up his pen in a gesture of dismissal.

I flounced out of the room and banged the door behind me, shaking with anger and well aware that my actions were childish, but quite unable to alter them. Suddenly the desire to see Edmund was overwhelming and, however unfitting it might be, I decided to ride into town on my own.

"Miss, what on earth's the matter with you? I've never known you to fidget so much."

Jess was trying to button me into my riding habit, and it was quite true—I couldn't keep still!

"My cousin is the most uncooperative person I've ever met!" My voice shook with anger. "He doesn't think it fitting that I should ride into town, and yet he refuses point-blank to accompany me."

Jess completed her task with a sigh of relief.

"Anyone who can refuse you so abruptly must have plenty of courage, I'd say."

She smiled in affectionate amusement, and I realized I was standing, hands on hips, my lips clamped together and my hair an untidy frame for my white face. I relaxed and sat on the bed, rubbing my hands wearily over my face.

"I don't know what's wrong with me," I said shakily. "I'm not usually so nervous."

"You must remember, miss, you've had a great loss in your life." Jess began to clear up my discarded clothes. "I think your cousin is right. You should be resting, not going into town."

I stood up quickly. "I'll go mad if I stay here with him!"

Jess shrugged, and I could see she would say no more on the subject, though her disapproval was apparent.

It was good to be outside, even though the mist was creeping more thickly across the fields by now. I went to the stables, and William looked at me in surprise.

"The coach isn't here, miss." His sleeves were rolled above his elbows, and I could see he was extremely busy.

"I'm sorry to make work for you, Will, but do you think you could get Puzzle saddled up for me? I have to go into town."

He stared at me in bewilderment.

"But the new boss—you know, Mr. Greyson—he's just been here and told me that no horses are to go out today. I'm sorry, miss."

I marched past him into the stable. "I'll do it myself, then. Mr. Greyson takes too much upon himself!"

I felt certain that my aunt would at least have given Puzzle to me. He had been mine ever since I was a child.

Will was like a cat on hot coals, not knowing what to do, and it was with profound relief that he informed me that my uncle was just turning into the gate. Will hurried forward to help unfasten the horses, and Uncle, smiling cheerfully, stepped out of the coach and came toward me.

"Why are you dressed like that, my dear? I hope you are not thinking of riding today? The mist is growing very thick."

He took my hand in his, and I found myself relaxing a little.

"I did want to go into town, Uncle. I have someone I wish to see there."

"Please don't think of riding in alone, Charlotte. I'll take you myself when I've had just a little rest and perhaps a glass or two of wine."

Feeling all sorts of a fool, I linked my arm with his and went back to the house with him.

"Go on; change into something nice, and we'll buy you a few bobs and bits to cheer you up." He smiled and brushed back my hair. "Humor an old man, my dear, and allow me to get some pretty green ribbons for those red curls."

He put his hand to his head and for a moment seemed a little unsteady on his feet.

"What is it, Uncle? Are you ill?"

Concerned, I helped him to a chair and quickly poured him some brandy. He leaned back and closed his eyes.

"Don't worry; I'll be all right in a few minutes. It's just the long journey from Wales and the strain of the funeral arrangements. It's all beginning to tell." He opened his eyes, and I could see that he was making an effort to smile. "I'm not so young as I was."

I suddenly felt quite ashamed of myself. What did it matter if I went to town today or next week? Probably Edmund had nothing of startling importance to tell me, anyway.

"You must rest this afternoon, Uncle," I said decisively, "and when you feel better, we'll take that trip into town, and you can buy me as many green ribbons as you like!"

I avoided Greyson as much as I could; it wasn't difficult. He was very much occupied with affairs of the estate and often ate his meals alone. Uncle Tom continued to feel the strain of the past days, and eventually he reluctantly agreed that I should go into town.

"Don't worry, Uncle," I told him. "Will knows the animals better than anyone in the stables. He even knows every pothole in the road, so you see I'll be fine."

To my embarrassment, he insisted that I take a purse full of money to spend, though I really had no intention of shopping at all.

"Thank you, Uncle; you are very kind."

Impulsively I bent to kiss his cheek and then hurried out into the sharp autumn air.

Will grinned cheerfully at me, and I smiled back.

"Nice crisp afternoon, Will," I said. "Let's put some speed into it once we're away from the gate."

He winked like a conspirator, and I knew he was as happy to be out for the afternoon as I was. We rode down the drive at a steady gait, but once on the road, Will gave the horses their head, and we bounced along at a cracking pace. I leaned out of the window, my teeth chattering together as we rode the bumps, enjoying every minute of it.

Suddenly the coach gave a tremendous lurch, there was an awful crunching sound, and I was flung to the floor. It seemed for a moment as if the coach would turn right over, but miraculously, the movement stopped, and I lay senseless for a moment, coming back to awareness with Will shaking me frantically.

"Oh, thank God you're alive, miss." He was white

and very shaken, and for a moment we sat in silence, looking at the disaster.

"One of the horses is dead, miss; broken neck, I think. It's a wonder we are not dead, too. One of the wheels has sheered right off."

I shook my head in an attempt to clear it.

"I suppose the accident was my fault, Will," I said soothingly. "If I hadn't urged you to go so fast, it probably wouldn't have happened."

He shook his head. "I crawled under to have a look, and I don't think it was an accident, miss. The side pieces have been cut halfway through."

I digested this information in silence. It couldn't be deliberate; it must have been a case of neglecting to renew whatever bits and pieces had rotted. I struggled to my feet with difficulty.

"The question is: What are we going to do now?" I said, wincing at the pain in my ankle.

"I've thought of that, miss," Will said quickly. "I reckon we're nearer to Winston than to town, so I'll walk back while you rest here. We'll soon get help for you."

I wasn't too thrilled at the prospect of spending an hour or two alone, but I didn't feel up to walking very far; and in any case, Will was young and strong.

"What about the other horse? Isn't he fit to ride?" I asked hopefully.

Will shook his head decidedly. "No, he's lame.

Don't think anything's broken, though. Don't worry, miss; I won't be long." He looked around ruefully. "I wish we'd picked a better spot for it," he said. "These trees make everything look darker, and I think it's coming on to rain again."

"Go on then, Will. The sooner you go, the sooner you'll send help back." I squeezed his arm. "Don't worry about me. I'm quite tough really."

He grinned cheekily. "We all know that, miss. We've heard you shouting often enough!"

He loped off, and I watched until he was out of sight and the road was an empty twisting band with no one on it but me.

I lifted my skirt to inspect my ankle. It was slightly swollen, but after pressing and exploring carefully with the tips of my fingers, I came to the conclusion that nothing much was wrong.

"Well, Edmund, it looks like our meeting is fated not to take place!" I said the words out loud, and they echoed among the trees, making me feel more alone than ever.

After a while, I became aware of the sound of a running stream. It didn't sound too far away, and the thought of a sweet fresh drink was very tempting. I could also take the opportunity to bathe my ankle, which by now felt three times its normal size.

Taking my time, I hobbled through grass and boulders, closing my eyes in relief when at last I saw the stream. The water trickling through my fingers was a delight, and so engrossed was I that for a moment the sound of horses didn't register. I heard voices back on the road, and as quickly as I could made my way back through the trees.

Darkness seemed to be falling swiftly, and I began to call out for fear that I wouldn't be seen. Finally I burst out onto the road and only then realized that these men could not have been sent to help me. There were roughly dressed, and one of them was brandishing a firearm.

"Take any money and jewelry, and let's get out of here," one of them said.

My arm was grasped roughly and twisted behind my back. I began to struggle but quickly realized how futile that was. I might just as well try to resist a wild bull! Instead, I slumped backwards as if in a faint, leaning heavily against the man. For a moment the man released me, and then I was away, forgetting the pain in my ankle, forgetting everything in my fright except the need to escape.

Surprise gave me the advantage, and I darted into the shelter of the trees, hearing shouts and the sound of stamping horses behind me. A shot that was frighteningly close spurred me on, though my heart was pounding as if it would burst, and I thought that at any moment I would fall into a faint.

Suddenly I felt myself grasped from behind, and

as a scream rose to my lips a hand covered my face, half smothering me. I expected to feel cold steel against me at any moment and stood still, paralyzed by fright.

Slowly I was turned around and, still held in an iron-like grip, was drawn slowly away from the road and further into the trees. Briefly I wondered if there was any point in struggling.

Abruptly I was released. Amazed, I turned to look at the man who towered above me. It was my cousin Greyson.

CHAPTER TWO

"Really, Uncle, I don't know why you are making such a fuss. I feel quite well this morning. There is no reason I should remain in bed."

All the same, I was quite enjoying the attention everyone was giving me. The doctor had bound up my ankle and seen to my bruises, and now, looking back on the experience from the comfort of my bed, the happenings of the previous night seemed to be almost an adventure.

"You'll do as you're told for once, my girl!" My uncle sat beside me, his smile softening the sternness of his words. "You've had a nasty shock. I knew I shouldn't have allowed you out alone."

I patted his hand. "Well, I'm all right now. But I still haven't seen Edmund. He'll wonder what's become of me."

My uncle looked at me from under his bushy white eyebrows, a smile crinkling the corners of his eyes.

"Ah, now I see what all the fuss was about! Why didn't you tell me you wanted to see the young man?" He got to his feet stiffly. "Old age doesn't come alone, so they say. I think I'll ask the doctor for a remedy before he leaves." He went to the door, pausing with his hand resting on his cane. "I'll have a message sent round to that young man of yours, and you can come down to the drawing room, for a treat, just for an hour or two."

"I shall enjoy that." I smiled as he left the room, amused at the way he insisted on treating me like a child.

There was an abrupt knock on the door, and Greyson let himself into the room. Color raced to my cheeks as I became aware of my tangled hair falling on to my shoulders and the plainness of my nightgown.

"I hope you are feeling all right," he said in a tone that didn't sound very solicitous. "As soon as possible you are to go down to Wales. I don't want too much delay."

"I'm sorry if my presence is an inconvenience!" The angry words tumbled out before I could think. "Probably you think last night's little episode was a plan to keep me longer at Winston!"

He sat down without any ceremony. "Don't be silly, Charlotte. You were very lucky to escape from that situation with your life."

I leaned back against the pillows. "Yes; I should thank you for that, I suppose. It was good of you to ride on ahead of the others."

I stared at him challengingly, but his expression didn't change.

"You flatter yourself, cousin. It was pure luck that I was riding that way at all!" He bowed his head over my hand. "Yet I admit the situation had its better moments."

The ready color came to my face again as I thought of the closeness with which he had held me.

"You might have been a little gentler in your handling of me!" I snapped. "At one stage I thought you were going to dispatch me yourself."

He rose and grinned down at me. "Perhaps I was tempted. You are not the sweetest person to be with." He moved toward the door. "The point of my visit is this. Early next week you must travel down to Wales. If my father isn't well enough to take you, I shall have to travel with you myself."

He nodded as if to emphasize his words and then, before I could think of a reply, went out, closing the door quietly behind him.

I dressed with special care that evening, more to please Uncle Tom than to impress Edmund. He'd known me in my tomboy days, when I'd done my utmost to beat him at climbing trees, and more often than not succeeded, too!

"There, your hair does look lovely, Miss Charlotte." Jess stood back to admire her handiwork, and

I had to agree that she had nimble fingers when it came to coaxing curls to stay in place.

"I'll do," I said, "though the effect will be spoiled by the fact that I'll have to limp into the room!"

"Just think of it this way, miss." Jess grinned mischievously. "All the gentlemen will rush to your side in order to help you to a chair."

I sighed. "That will most likely be Uncle Tom. Edmund lacks the imagination. And I can't see my cousin Greyson rushing to help anyone."

I was wrong. When I entered the drawing room, Edmund and Greyson reached me almost simultaneously, and smiling to myself, I leaned on both their arms.

"You look very beautiful, Charlotte." My uncle beamed at me from his chair beside the fire. His normally ruddy cheeks were pale, and he seemed to have a slightly pinched expression on his face.

"Thank you, Uncle; its kind of you to say so." I went forward to have a quiet word with him while Greyson attended to the wine. "Are you feeling all right, Uncle? You look a little pale."

He waved my concern aside. "Of course I'm all right. Now stop worrying and enjoy yourself. I'm feeling the cold, that's all."

He might have been right, because after a few drinks his color returned and he began to look more relaxed.

Edmund seemed to be more than a little uneasy. Several times I tried to sit beside him and engage him in conversation, but he appeared to avoid any direct questions I put to him. It seemed only a few minutes before he rose and made his apologies for having to leave so early.

"Pressure of work, you know," he said with a brightness that was quite out of place.

Greyson rose, too. "In the circumstances, Charlotte, I will see your friend out."

To my annoyance, Edmund quickly agreed. "Yes, of course; no need to disturb yourself, Charlotte. You rest that foot as much as possible."

Greyson returned a few minutes later and poured himself another drink.

"Nervous chap, that friend of yours. He looked at me as if I had two heads or something. Couldn't get away quickly enough."

"The whole evening had a damper on it," I thought," I said quickly. "You may be right, Greyson. It could be due to your peculiarities."

I saw by the flash of anger in his eyes that I'd struck home, but he wasn't going to let matters rest there.

"No doubt you have grown accustomed to entertaining men alone, but it isn't the correct way to behave."

I smiled with false sweetness. "Why, cousin, I

hadn't realized what a nasty turn of mind you have."

Near the fire, Uncle Tom stirred, our raised voices apparently have brought him out of his doze.

"What are you two quarreling about now? Can't an old man have some peace?" He struggled to his feet. "I'm going to my bed. I'll leave you to your disagreements."

As he made his way to the door, I hobbled after him.

"Wait for me, Uncle. Greyson thinks it's terribly wrong for me to be alone with him."

I looked back over my shoulder, but my cousin had turned his back and was pouring himself more wine, quite oblivious to my attempts at sarcasm.

I had begun to think that a meeting alone with Edmund would be impossible when Uncle asked me to accompany him into town.

"We can look around the shops a little. I need an hour to myself to conclude some business matters, but after that, we can enjoy ourselves. Would you like that, Charlotte?"

Greyson quite obviously wasn't taken with the idea. He stood, hands thrust into his pockets, glowering at me.

"I don't think a trip into town is a good thing just now, Father, as you haven't been feeling very well lately."

"I'll be all right." Uncle Tom smiled. "It's a splendid day. And in any case, I can buy some remedies from the excellent shop in the High Street."

Greyson said no more, and shortly afterward, the coach was brought around to the front. It was with an almost childish feeling of excitement that I followed my uncle out into the morning brightness.

The tang of autumn was enlivening the air, and the leaves were shades of copper and red, ready to fall at the slightest breath of wind.

"This must surely be your season," Uncle Tom remarked as Will drove slowly through the gate. "With that bright hair of yours, you are a perfect picture."

I was happy to see there was color in his cheeks this morning.

"I'm sure you are flattering me out of kindness, Uncle," I said, smiling, "but I won't pretend I don't enjoy it."

Soon we had reached the cobbled streets of the town, and I couldn't help comparing the calm uneventful journey with the strange happenings of my last one. I smiled happily. Now I would surely find the opportunity to ask Edmund the reason for his hastily scribbled message.

"Enjoy yourself, Charlotte. But don't walk about too much on that ankle. It still isn't strong, you know." Uncle Tom kissed my cheek lightly. "I'll be at the banker's if you need me."

As I stood there in the crisp sunshine, watching him walk away, I felt a sudden ache of affection for him. He was the father I'd never had, and he looked so frail that I wondered if Greyson had been right after all in disapproving of the trip.

In any event, it was too late to think of that now. I was in town, and I might as well enjoy myself.

Edmund's office was a small, dusty room just off the High Street. No sunshine ever seemed to penetrate the windows, and there was always an intriguing smell of leather permeating the place.

He opened the door, an expression of surprise on his honest face.

"Hello, Edmund. Aren't you going to invite me inside?"

I didn't wait for his answer. I knew from experience that he wasn't given to quick replies.

"What are you doing here, Charlie?" He used his old childhood nickname for me, and I smiled at him warmly, wondering if it was the unexpected sunshine that had put me in such a good humor.

"Your note," I said briefly. "Well, what was it all about?"

I seated myself firmly in his large leather-bound chair, resting my arms on the scratched surface of his desk.

"My note?" His brow furrowed, and I sighed in

exasperation.

I took the crumpled paper from my pocket. "You gave this to Jess for me, isn't that right? It says, 'Come to my office; I must see you.' Well, here I am."

Edmund sat down opposite me. He was obviously struggling for words. I almost laughed at his comic expression of embarrassment.

"I was hasty in sending you that note, Charlotte. Since then, matters have been explained to my satsifaction."

"Well, not to mine!" I said angrily. "Edmund, I wish to know what Aunt Grace said about me in her will. She couldn't have neglected me altogether."

"Leave things alone," Edmund said abstractedly. "There is nothing of importance; merely a few trinkets and such. Your cousin is the rightful heir, I assure you of that."

"Can't you show me the will?" I smiled as charmingly as I knew how, and Edmund swallowed with difficulty.

"I don't have it now."

He stared miserably at me, expecting me to fly off the handle as I usually did. But there was no point in that now. Edmund was as honest as anyone could be, and if he gave his word that Aunt Grace had left everything in Greyson's name, he must be telling the truth.

"Thank you, Edmund." With a sigh, I got to my feet and walked disconsolately to the door. Edmund came across to me and put his hand gently on my arm.

"Why don't you marry me, Charlie? You know I'll look after you."

For a moment, looking into his eyes shining with admiration, I was very tempted to say yes and take the easy way out. True, I wouldn't be living at Winston, but I would still be in the vicinity.

Taking advantage of my hesitation, he bent forward, and for a moment, his lips were warm on mine.

I drew away and shook my head.

"I'm not ready for marriage, Edmund, though I'm aware of the honor you pay me. Anyway, think of the life you'd have with me having a tantrum every five minutes!"

He smiled. "I won't give up, Charlotte. I'll keep asking you. One day you may say yes."

I inclined my head. "You could be right about that. For now I must be free. But thank you for everything, Edmund."

I found myself out in the sunshine once more, walking aimlessly along the street, my cheeks burning, wondering why I hadn't said a quick yes to Edmund. It wasn't every day that I received a proposal from an eligible young man, and only a few short weeks before I'd imagined it was just what I was waiting for.

"Hey, wake up; you're in another world." Uncle Tom was standing before me, his face wreathed in smiles. "What on earth did that young man say to make you look like this?"

I linked my arm with his and smiled mischievously. "For one thing, he proposed to me! A very nice compliment, you must agree."

I felt my uncle stiffen. He stopped walking and looked down at me in consternation. "You haven't accepted?" His tone was sharp. I looked at him in surprise.

"Why, no; as a matter of fact, I haven't. But why? What's wrong?"

He squeezed my arm. "I'm a selfish old man, my dear. I've been so looking forward to taking you to Wales that the thought of you getting married and remaining here really gave me a turn."

Indeed, he did look quite pale, and his hand shook as it rested on mine.

"Well, I refused him; but I didn't burn my boats! I'm too cautious for that!" I said, and laughed, hoping to cheer him.

"Very wise, I'm sure, Charlotte; in Wales there will be plenty of young men for you to meet. I'd like to keep you near me if possible."

"You are very sweet, Uncle," I said softly, "and I'll certainly look over these eligible young men you are going to introduce me to. But I'm warning you

36

now: I'm not yet ready for marriage, in spite of my age!"

We went back to the carriage then. Uncle Tom seemed to be quite exhausted, and my own spirits were low; I looked forward to some good hot tea.

"Here, my dear; a little something I promised you."

As we settled ourselves into the seats, Uncle Tom handed me a small parcel, and a lump came to my throat as a riot of green ribbons tumbled onto my skirts.

CHAPTER THREE

"Goodbye. Be sure to take care of yourself." I leaned out of the carriage window and kissed my uncle's cheek. "I won't rest until you are fit enough to join me in Wales. I'm going to be so lonely."

Will urged the horses forward, and I leaned out of the window, waving my handkerchief, until we were well out of the gate and Winston disappeared from sight behind the trees. I sat back, pretending the sharp wind had brought tears to my eyes.

"We'll be back for visits, Miss Charlotte," Jess said comfortingly, not at all fooled by my pretense. Greyson didn't even bother to comment, but sat upright and bored, his eyes on the passing countryside.

"I doubt that, Jess," I said sharply. "We wouldn't be welcome."

We stopped to eat at one of the many coaching inns that were spread about the countryside like mushrooms in the early morning, and Jess asked my permission to ride up front with William, once we'd finished our meal.

"Yes, go ahead; I'd join you myself if I could,"

I said sulkily. Jess's crestfallen face suddenly brought back my good humor. "Go on, flirt with your Will; I don't blame you a bit. He's better company than you'll find on the inside of the coach."

"And so say all of us," murmured Greyson, opening a book and holding it up in front of his face.

If I hadn't been so angry I would have laughed. Instead, I sniffed my disapproval and leaned back, closing my eyes and trying my level best to fall asleep. I must have succeeded, because the next thing I knew, Greyson was shaking my arm.

"You have slept for hours," he said smugly. "I think you are going to have some difficulty getting any sleep tonight."

Bewildered, I looked out to find that we were in the courtyard of another inn, and by now the sky was darkening to a deep purple.

"It's your scintillating conversation that does it," I said sharply. My head ached, and my throat and mouth felt dry. I shivered as I hurried through the door and made directly for the blazing fire.

I couldn't face eating much supper, though Greyson didn't notice; he was obviously very hungry. I deliberately turned my eyes away from his plate—the thought of eating nauseated me, and my face felt as if it were on fire.

"You look a bit feverish," Greyson remarked indifferently. "Don't you think it would be a good idea for you to go to bed?"

I rose immediately, and the room seemed to swim around me. I tried to make a dignified exit, but Greyson caught my arm and insisted on leading me to my room.

"I'll send Jess to you," he said. "Probably you've caught a chill. I hope it won't prevent you from traveling."

Weakly I sat on the edge of the bed. "Oh, don't worry about that. I'll be fit to travel, even if I've got to crawl."

I glared at him, and to my surprise he smiled and sat beside me, his hand suddenly cool against my forehead.

"You remind me of a little goat, butting against anything that gets in your way." There was laughter in his voice.

"I'm always happy to be a source of amusement," I said, strangely disturbed by his closeness.

"Prickly little Charlotte. You are funny." He caught my face in his hands and turned me toward him. Then his lips were warm on mine, and unaccountably, my heart was racing.

He moved away. "I'll send a hot drink for you. Keep warm, that's the main thing," he said, and grinned as he went to the door. "I think my own temperature has risen somewhat in the last few minutes."

I kicked off my shoes and put my feet up on the bed, my head a jumble of confused thoughts. Was it possible I'd misjudged Greyson? He was certainly very attractive in a dark, lean way.

Jess came into the room, a steaming cup in her hand.

"Are you all right, miss?" She fussed around opening the buttons on my dress and wryly I submitted to her ministrations.

"To tell the truth, Jess, I'm aching in every bone. What's that you've got there?"

She smiled mysteriously. "I persuaded the landlord to allow me to make up a brew of herbs for you. It will reduce your fever; and Mr. Greyson says that's what's needed if we are to push on tomorrow."

I sipped the bitter liquid dutifully. "Oh, Mr. Greyson won't be inconvenienced; he needn't worry about that," I said, angry with him all over again, and angry at myself that I'd allowed a few kind words and a kiss to blind me to the fact that he was turning me out of my home.

I snuggled down, warming my feet gratefully against the hot water bottle Jess had managed to find.

"I'll be better in the morning," I said sleepily. "Blow out the candle Jess, there's a good girl."

To my surprise, I did feel slightly better when I

awoke to find the sun streaming into my room. I even managed to eat a light breakfast and then pinched some color into my cheeks to hide my paleness before joining Greyson outside in the courtyard.

"How are you feeling, Charlotte?"

His eyes were shrewd as they searched my face, but I bustled past him and got into the welcome shelter of the coach. The morning breeze was fresher than I'd realized.

"I'll be all right," I said coolly, deliberately avoiding his gaze. Drawing my cloak around me, I settled back, keeping well away from the window.

"So, Jess, you are not riding with Will this morning?" I deliberately made my voice cheerful, though my throat had begun to ache once more.

"No fear, miss. The wind's too nippy. I know when I'm well off."

I did my best to smile, then leaned back and closed my eyes. Greyson was still watching me, and I didn't feel up to having an argument with him just then.

"Are you sure you do not want to turn back?" he said quite pleasantly. "A day or two will make little difference."

I shook my head without answering, and after a while I could tell by the rustle of paper that he was reading one of his books again.

As the day wore on, I began to feel really ill. I could scarcely hold my head up, but I said nothing, determined not to be the cause of delaying the journey.

Slowly the countryside was beginning to change, and the horses were forced to labor up steep slopes. At last we came to such a difficult pass that Greyson decided we'd better leave the coach so as to lighten the burden on the animals. The wind seemed piercingly cold at such high altitudes, and as I struggled with the unevenness of the ground, there was a sudden ringing in my ears. And then I was slipping down, with blackness all around me. . . .

Greyson was carrying me then. I dimly felt his arms wing me up and place me inside the coach, and Jess, her face white, swung her own thick brown cloak around my shoulders.

"What's wrong?" I struggled to sit up, but Greyson urged me back against the seat.

"Sit still, you little fool. Why on earth didn't you say you were feeling so ill? Do you enjoy being a martyr?"

I didn't bother to answer him; all I wanted was a comfortable bed so that I could stretch my weary bones in comfort. I felt Jess shiver beside me and noticed, as if through a mist, that she had no cloak.

Jess, put something on or you'll be ill, too!" I croaked, indicating that she take something from the bag on the seat beside me. Her cloak, though rough, was thick and warm around me, and it seemed too much trouble for me to move to take it off again.

She did as she was told and, even through my discomfort, I could see she felt like a queen in my soft green velvet. She was welcome to it. I was quite happy as I was.

I closed my eyes, dozing intermittently, only waking when I heard Greyson call out some instruction to Will, or when Jess moved to stretch her legs beside me.

"It isn't much farther," Greyson said softly. "It looks as if she'll be laid up for a few days, silly girl."

Suddenly it was as if the world were exploding. I sat up, wondering if I was delirious with fever; but again there was a volley of shots from outside the coach and a great deal of shouting.

A face appeared in the window, and I heard Jess give a thin scream before the door was flung open and she was dragged out into the darkness.

Weakly I struggled to my feet and lurched out into the road. I saw the glint of a knife as it descended in an arc and struck viciously at Jess. The wind screamed, taking away my thin voice, and then I pitched forward onto the road.

Something was hurting my cheek. Gingerly I lifted my head and saw I'd been resting heavily against a sharp boulder. It was still dark, and the wind still screamed along the narrow ridge of the road. For an awful moment I thought I was the only one alive in the whole world. I struggled to sit up and heard a moan somewhere to my left.

"Will? Greyson? Who is it?"

Vainly I tried to pierce the intense darkness with my eyes, edging forward cautiously, not feeling the sharpness of the stones beneath my hands.

"Miss, are you all right?"

Will's voice was close to me, and when I put out my hand I touched the warmth of his.

"Oh, Will, what's happened? Eagerly I grasped his arm. "Have we had an accident?"

Then the awful memory flooded back of Jess pitching forward into a crumpled heap on the ground. I stifled a scream and covered my mouth with my hand.

"Listen, miss, I can hear the horses; they can't be too far off. Just sit still, and I'll go and find them."

In the darkness I huddled alone, tears of shock and fear wet on my cold cheeks. I was terrified to think what had happened. I didn't know if Greyson had been killed. There was certainly no sign of him.

"Miss Charlotte, where are you?" Will's voice came thin and flat through the sound of the wind, and with difficulty, I forced myself to stand and move toward him.

"Here, Will. Here I am. Have you found anything?"

Thankfully I heard the clip-clop of horses' hooves

and the creak of the coach as Will drew nearer.

"Come on, miss; I'll light the lanterns, and we'll see what's what."

He helped me into the warmth of the coach, and then suddenly everything was illuminated. There was dried blood on Will's forehead—he'd obviously been struck a vicious blow by someone, and he was as pale as death.

"I cannot see any reason for it, miss," he said in bewilderment. "I thought they were highwaymen, but see! Nothing's been taken."

He was right. The baggage was still stowed away in the compartment, and I still had my jewelry in the bag at my side.

"I'll take a look outside, miss."

Will moved away, and I could see the lantern bobbing through the darkness. My mouth was dry as I waited for his return, hoping against all reason that Jess was all right. I didn't even allow myself to think of Greyson. There had been such a lot of shots fired that he could be lying out in the darkness, fatally wounded.

Will returned, and I saw at once that he was very distressed. I helped him inside the coach, and he sat for a moment, his head in his hands, his thin young shoulders heaving.

"Oh, Will, what is it?"

I sat beside him, my arms around him, trying my

best to comfort him. He didn't need to speak; I knew already the answer to my questions.

"It's Jess, miss. She's dead. Those murderous villains have killed her!"

My head was spinning, and there was a bitter taste of tears on my lips.

"But why should anyone want to kill Jess? It doesn't make sense."

"They thought it was *you*, miss." Will pulled himself together and looked at me, his eyes clear. "Jess was wearing your cloak, don't you see?"

My blood ran cold. I could feel the color leave my face. In the lamplight, I looked down at myself, covered from head to toe in the thick brown cloak Jess had given me to keep me warm. And now she was out there in the darkness, dead, wearing my green velvet.

"You must be right, Will. She would be mistaken for me. But I don't know who would want me dead." My voice quivered, and suddenly I could bear it all no longer. "Get us away from here, Will, I beg of you. Someone will be sent to see to Jess and to look for Mr. Greyson as soon as we get to the next inn."

Will shook his head. "There's no sign of Mr. Greyson, miss. Perhaps they've taken him off." He shrugged his shoulders. "We might never learn what they were up to."

The rest of the journey was a nightmare. There

were times when, mercifully, I lapsed into uncon-
sciousness; and in between, I cried bitter and helpless
tears.

I opened my eyes in a strange room. The pale sun
slanted in through the small windows, showing small
notes of dust whirling in the slanting rays of light.
I sat up, aware that the fever had left me. I felt tired
and weak, but completely in control of my senses.

The door opened quietly, and Greyson walked into
the room, his arm bound and a long cut stretching
across his brow. We stared at each other in silence
for a long moment, and then he came and sat beside
me on the bed.

"Charlotte, that was a terrible thing to have happen. I can't tell you how sorry I am."

I'd never seen him without a glint of amusement
in his eyes before, and the effect on me was strangely
disturbing.

"We did our best, Will and I, but there were too
many of them. And they were armed. I didn't protect
you very well, did I?"

I struggled to sit up. "You can't possibly blame
yourself. And don't worry about me; I wasn't hurt
at all." Tears misted my eyes. "I can't forget Jess,
so still there in the darkness." I shuddered. "It was
horrible!"

Greyson caught my hand. "Try not to think about

it; rest assured I'll find out what it was all about somehow."

A sudden thought struck me. "But what happened to you? Will searched for you without success." Greyson shrugged. "I was there all right. He must have missed me in the darkness. I expect I was unconscious." There was a glimpse of the old derision in his eyes. "I didn't expect to wake up and find myself on a mountain alone."

"I'm sorry, Greyson; I was so frightened I couldn't think straight. Were you hurt badly?" I looked with concern at the bandage on his arm.

"No, it's nothing to worry about; it won't stop us from going on as soon as you feel fit enough. It's not far now, and I know you'll love Plas Melyn. At least I think I can guarantee you'll be safe from attack there."

My hackles rose. He was still concerned only with getting rid of me and returning to Winston, in spite of all that had happened.

"I'm fit now," I said briskly. "All that was wrong with me was a chill, and I've a strong constitution; so please make arrangements to resume the journey as soon as possible."

He rose abruptly. "Very well, Charlotte." He seemed relieved and quite unaware of my animosity. "This is one journey I'll be happy to see truly over."

I struggled with my tears as I climbed out of bed.

Soon I'd be left like an unwanted parcel in a strange home, with no one to confide in and no one to seek comfort from. I could only pray that Uncle Tom would return to his home as quickly as possible.

As the coach stopped before the ornate gates of Plas Melyn, even I had to admit that it was a truly beautiful place. The large house, with its attractive turrets, sprawled along the banks of the estuary, and soft green gardens stretched peacefully down to the water's edge.

"Plas Melyn," Greyson said, and the pride in his voice was quite clear for anyone to hear. "See the twin suns figured in the ironwork of the gates? From those the house takes its name: Yellow Mansion."

"It's lovely!" I spoke spontaneously and immediately wondered why on earth Greyson should want to leave such a home to go to live in strange surroundings.

The interior was opulent, the carpets rich and multi-colored, and the furniture gleamed warmly. The staff lined up to greet our arrival, and most of them smiled pleasantly enough at me, no doubt curious about the "poor relation" who was being given a home.

My own rooms were above reproach, far more sumptuous than the ones I'd lived in at Winston, and from each window, there was a breathtaking view of the sea lapping gently against the shore.

Greyson stood patiently waiting for me to make some comment. I turned and looked directly at him.

"Why do you want to live at Winston, when there's all this?"

He didn't answer; he just placed my bags on the floor and turned to go.

"Make yourself comfortable, Charlotte," he said, and his voice was quite impersonal. "Remember, this is *your* home now."

Shortly after he left there was a knock on the door, and a young rosy-cheeked maid stood aside to admit William. He hesitated for a moment on the threshold.

"Come inside, Will. I'm glad to see you." I closed the door and pulled across a thick velvet curtain that had been strategically placed to keep out any draught. "Is there anything I can do for you?"

He fidgeted nervously for a moment. "I don't rightly know how to say this, miss." He hesitated before taking a deep breath and plunging into speech. "I think Mr. Greyson had something to do with the attack on the road."

The words had spilled out and hung like frightened sheep in the silence of the room. I stared at him in amazement, not making sense of anything he said.

"Sit down, Will. I know Jess's death upset you."

I rubbed my hand tiredly across my eyes, and Will continued to stand uncomfortably near the door.

"His arm, miss—it's not real bad. I was helping him unload the trunks, and he could swing them down as easy as I could."

I digested this in silence. If what Will said was true, it certainly seemed odd. But then maybe he'd just had a sprain and not a wound as I'd imagined.

"Not only that, miss, but I overheard something funny." He stopped and I gestured impatiently for him to go on. "The night the villains attacked the coach, I heard one of them say plain as anything that Mr. Greyson wasn't to be harmed."

I stood up and went over to him. "I'm sure there's a perfectly sound explantion; but just the same, keep it to yourself."

He went to the door. "Well, miss, I'm to go back to Winston tomorrow. Not that I like leaving you here alone."

"You mean Mr. Greyson is returning so quickly?" I asked abruptly.

Will shook his head. "No, miss. I'm to take the coach alone, just in case your uncle wants to use it."

"Well, take care then, Will; and you can take a letter to my uncle for me. The sooner he arrives here, the better I'll feel."

After Will had gone, I sat looking around me listlessly, not knowing what to do. I supposed I could occupy myself unpacking my luggage. Before the resolution was clear in my mind, there was another knock on the door, and a young girl came into the room, bobbing politely to me.

"Mr. Greyson sent me to see to your things," she said. "And I'm to ask you to take some wine with him in the drawing room."

To my surprise, Greyson had someone with him as I entered. She raised her head gracefully, her blue eyes scrutinizing me with an excess of curiosity.

"Ah, Charlotte, I want you to meet Wenna."

Greyson came forward, playing the part of a dutiful cousin prefectly, and led me to the sofa.

"What a charming name," I said, giving her back look for look. "I presume it is Welsh in origin?"

She inclined her head in a regal gesture without actually speaking, and at once I felt like an impertinent child.

"Wenna runs the house for Father," he said quickly. "I don't know what we'd do without her."

The smile he gave her was warmer than her services merited, and for a moment her icy eyes seemed to glow.

"Oh, you mean a sort of housekeeper?" I remarked pointedly. "Did someone mention a glass of wine?"

I waited while Greyson poured the sparkling ruby drink into my glass. "Have you been here long,

Wenna?" I looked her over, from her well-groomed hair that was touched with grey to her feet. "I expect you have."

Greyson laughed uncomfortably. "Don't make her sound like part of the furniture, Charlotte. Wenna is a very important person, believe me. As I said, we couldn't manage without her."

CHAPTER FOUR

It was strange preparing for bed in the large luxurious room, with the sound of the incoming tide just a few floors below me.

I stood for a moment looking across the moon-silvered water, noticing for the first time that there was a tiny island in the middle of the estuary. A light bobbed unevenly, as if someone holding a lantern were stumbling in the darkness; and then suddenly it was extinguished. I shrugged. Maybe there were fishermen out laying their nets. In any case, it was no concern of mine.

I slipped into bed, feeling strange and miserable, wishing with all my heart I were home at Winston.

"I hope you are going to come to the chapel with us Charlotte."

Wenna stood, her head tipped to one side, looking stunning all in black.

It was my first Sunday in Wales, and I could hear

the bell peal out as it had done since early morning.
"Yes, of course," I said. "I'll get my cloak."

As I moved toward the stairs, Wenna held out her
hand to stop me.

"That won't be necessary. We at the Plas worship
on our own grounds."

I had no idea what she meant, but Greyson came
from the drawing room just then and held out his
arms to Wenna and me. Deliberately I ignored his
gesture and followed them out into the crisp cold
sunshine.

Greyson did his best to include me in the conversation as we made our way through the gardens, but
I made it clear I was not in the mood to be drawn,
and after a few attempts, he left me alone.

The chapel was delightfully tiny, yet beautifully
proportioned. The bell that had irritated me with its
insistent ringing at daybreak now sounded mellow,
with the sun striking in all directions from its gleaming brass.

"Beautiful, isn't it?" Wenna stopped so suddenly
that I almost bumped into her. "It used to ring to
warn ships of the danger of high ground when the
tide was in full flood. But of course there's no need
of that now."

I managed a smile. "Why not?" I asked, trying not
to sound too curious.

Wenna shrugged. "The straits are avoided now.

Too many ships came to grief here. This chapel was often used to lay out the drowned seamen."

I shuddered as we went from the sunshine into the small interior of the building. Light fell through the stained glass windows like pools of blood on the oak floors, and I shook myself for being a silly imaginative fool.

The service was spoken entirely in Welsh, and though the strange musical intonations fascinated me for a time, I soon grew restless and bored.

Then suddenly it was over, and Greyson stood aside to let us lead the way outside.

"Well, Charlotte, what did you think of it?" Greyson took my arm in a light but firm grip, so that without making a scene I could not pull free.

"Very beautiful. But, of course, the fine words were lost on me. I didn't understand one word of it."

Unasked, Wenna came to my side. "It is a great pity, especially when you consider that your mother was Welsh."

I looked at her sharply, and I saw Greyson shake his head. Wenna colored slightly, and before I could speak she moved on ahead.

"Excuse me; I must see if everything is under control."

She smiled formally and went swiftly across the soft grass, tall and beautiful in her black dress.

"What does she know about my mother?" I asked

sharply, and Greyson looked down at me in surprise.
"Nothing very significant, I should think. Didn't
Aunt Grace ever tell you about her?"

I shook my head. "Nothing at all. The only thing
she did tell me was that both my parents were dead."

Greyson nodded. "Well, there was really nothing
more to be said then, was there?"

I glared at him angrily, knowing full well that he
was avoiding the issue.

"Mother used to live here, I presume?" I stood
right in front of him so that he was forced to look
down at me.

"Persistent little thing, aren't you?" The laughter
was in his eyes again, and I felt like kicking him
sharply on the shins. He took my arm and pulled
me forward. "Don't make a fool of yourself in front
of the staff and my visitors," he said calmly. "You
don't want them to think the English are a lot of hooli-
gans, do you?"

"What visitors?" I said, quickly glancing over his
shoulder.

"We always have visitors on Sunday. How else do
you think we fill our little chapel?"

He smiled and walked on, safe now in the knowledge that I would follow him.

The enormous dining table gleamed redly in the
afternoon sun, and the babble of voices talking in
a foreign tongue offended my ears. Greyson sat well

away from me, and I glared at him frequently, determined that on future occasions I would eat alone in my room rather than endure this.

As soon as Greyson gave the signal to move, I hurried up to my room, closing the door gratefully behind me.

Wearily, I went into the bedroom and leaned my head against the cool panes of the window. Quite a breeze had blown up, and I could see the water swirling angrily around the little island. It was strange, but I hadn't noticed before that there was a grave. Yet now, unmistakably, a cross stood out against the darkening sky.

I moved away and sat on the bed, loosening my shoes and curling my toes toward the fire.

There was a tap on the door, and without waiting for my answer, Wenna entered. I was not very pleased at the intrusion, but she was smiling, and in her hands was a tray of tea.

"I'm sorry to disturb you, Charlotte, but you looked a little overwrought downstairs. Are you all right?"

She sat down at the table, and I clenched my hands together in anger, resenting her patronizing tone.

"I'm quite all right," I said quietly. "But it was kind of you to bring me tea. Won't you join me?"

It was obvious that she had every intention of joining me, as there were two cups on the tray. She inclined her head graciously and began to pour.

Over my cup, I studied her smooth face. Everything she did, every movement suggested serenity; but there had to be some chink in her defense, and I believed I'd found it.

"You are in love with Greyson, aren't you?" I said bluntly. Rich color swept to her cheeks, and her eyes met mine with more than a glint of anger in them.

"I don't really see that it's any concern of yours, Charlotte." Her tone was pleasant, but the warning in it was quite plain.

"I agree," I said, "but my mother is. What do you know about her?"

She stood abruptly and looked down at me almost pityingly. Her hands as they brushed the front of her dress were steady and white against the black velvet.

"She was a maid here at the Plas. Are you satisfied now?"

There was no triumph in her voice; just a plain statement of fact. I looked at her in astonishment, and she must have seen the disbelief written all over my face.

"Greyson didn't want you to know, though there is no shame in being a servant. I'm one myself."

"My father married a servant, then?" I looked searchingly at her, and she shrugged.

"There is no record of any marriage. It would have been here in the chapel."

I took a quick drink of tea. No wonder Aunt Grace had refused to talk about my parents. She was ashamed that I was her brother's illegitimate child.

"Thank you for telling me," I said quietly.

My legs were trembling as I walked across to the window. There was nothing more to be said about the matter.

"Why, that's strange!" I pointed to the island, and Wenna came to my side quickly.

"What's wrong?" Her voice was breathless as she looked toward the island. "I can't see anything."

"Well, that's the point!" I said excitedly. "There was a cross there earlier, when I first came up from the dining room."

She was chalk-white as she studied my face. "That's silly rubbish!" she exclaimed. "You've been listening to the servants' gossip."

"A fat lot of good that would do me," I said angrily. "I can't understand a word they say."

She rubbed her eyes with her hand and stared toward the island. "Then you must have imagined it. A trick of the light or something." She went away from the window and rang the service bell. "I think we'd better have more tea."

"What's wrong, Wenna?" My tone was abrupt. "I saw a cross out there as plainly as I see you now, and last night I saw someone with a lantern. I'm not given to an excess of imagination, I assure you."

She shook her head. "It's nothing; there must be a logical explanation." She looked up at me, strangely fragile in that moment. "They do say the island is haunted, but that's just gossip, of course."

I shivered. "I didn't see any ghosts, I'm sure of that!" I warmed my hands before the fire. "Is there any way of getting across to the island?"

She nodded absent-mindedly. "Oh, yes, at low tide anyone can walk out there. But no one does." She had no authority to tell me not to go to the island, but her eyes were pleading. "Leave well alone Charlotte, please."

We stared at each other for a moment in silence, and then there was a light tap on the door. Wenna rose swiftly and with obvious relief.

"Ah, there's our tea."

Winter was beginning to paint icy fingers across the lovely Welsh mountains, and still my uncle had not come down from Winston. I was extremely worried about him. Even Greyson began to talk about going up there to see how he was.

I still hadn't found an opportunity to explore the island, but the determination was strong inside me. I stood at the quay and looked out to it. There just had to be an explanation for what I'd seen, and I would find out what it was.

The island rose from the sea like the back of a wet

brown dog. Startled, I realized there was someone on it—a still figure, tall, in a long black dress, and it looked like Wenna! I raised my arm and waved, but there was no answering gesture.

The wind lifted the woman's skirts, and I could see her hair streaming out behind her, dark and waist-length. She didn't move, and after a while, I began to shiver.

Suddenly frightened, I hurried back up the slippery slopes of the garden and into the warmth of the house. Wenna was standing at Greyson's side, her hair in its usual neat bun on the nape of her neck.

"What's wrong, Charlotte?" Greyson came and took my shaking hands in his warm ones, drawing me toward the fire. "Go and get her something hot," he said crisply, and at once Wenna obeyed. "What is it?"

Greyson lifted my face to his, and suddenly the events of the last weeks seemed too much. I threw myself into his arms and sobbed like a hysterical child. Gently he smoothed back my wind-blown hair, holding me close to him.

"You are safe with me, Charlotte," he whispered softly, and slowly, he tipped my face until he could kiss me. "You will always be safe with me."

There was a discreet cough, and as I self-consciously disengaged myself from Greyson's arms,

Wenna handed me a cup, her face blank.

"Thank you." I sat down in the nearest chair. "I don't know what came over me. I'm sorry to be so silly."

Greyson sat beside me, his hand caressing my hair. "What frightened you, Charlotte? You can tell me." There was no laughter in his eyes now; in fact, he seemed tense, much more so than the situation merited.

I shrugged. "I don't know. Nothing, I suppose. I'm homesick. Yes, that's all."

He stood up. "All right, if you won't tell me, then I can't make you, but I wish you trusted me a little more."

For several days the sun seemed to forget that it was winter and shone warmly, dispelling the snow from all but the topmost peaks of the mountains.

My good spirits seemed to return with the warmth, and I spent a great deal of time walking about the gardens, exploring the little tree house and the dovecote, which at the moment seemed absent of any birds at all.

I felt sure that now Uncle Tom would make the journey from Winston, and I wasn't at all surprised when I heard the big front gate creak open and the sound of a horse and carriage on the path.

"Charlotte," Greyson called, but I was already

running up from the garden toward the front of the house. It wasn't my uncle, but it was the next best thing.

"Edmund!" I shouted his name, glorying in the sight of his bright hair blowing in the breeze.

"Charlie!" He ran toward me and almost threw me into the air in his excitement.

Greyson came and stood like a tall dark shadow, towering over both of us.

"Won't you come inside?" he said coldly.

CHAPTER FIVE

Edmund had brought me a present, a gorgeous white, fluffy kitten with turquoise eyes. We sat in the drawing room, and I couldn't stop smiling, so delighted was I to see Edmund again.

"How's Uncle Tom?" I asked, smoothing the kitten's soft fur. It stretched tiny claws and then curled up to sleep.

"He is improving, though he did have a slight cold some weeks ago." Edmund leaned forward, glancing around the room to make sure we were alone. "He is concerned about you. He insisted he should be here instead of Greyson. Why don't you return with me to Winston?"

"That is out of the question!"

Edmund and I jumped guiltily as Greyson walked into the room. He poured himself some wine and with perfect manners refilled my glass, then Edmund's.

"I think you are both forgetting that this is now Charlotte's home." Greyson lifted his glass. "Winston belongs to me."

"No one is likely to forget that!" I said sharply. "You go to great pains to remind me constantly."

Edmund touched my arm, and when I looked at him I noticed that his color had risen.

"Charlotte could always become my wife," he said. "True, she wouldn't own Winston, but my home is comfortable, and I am well able to provide for her."

Greyson smiled a little. "Are you asking my permission? It really is none of my business, of course, but I think Charlotte is too immature to make a good wife for anyone right now."

"You are right," I said quickly. "It is none of your business." I glared at him angrily. "Is it too much to ask for a little privacy in what you keep telling me is 'my home'?"

Greyson nodded. "I see your point, cousin. Please continue your conversation. I will not disturb you again."

At once Edmund took me in his arms. "Please say you'll marry me, Charlotte. You know as well as I do it was always intended."

Gently I disengaged myself from his arms. "I'm afraid my cousin is right about one thing." I smiled to soften my words. "I am not ready for marriage yet—to anyone."

Edmund looked at me shrewdly. "Charlotte, you are not falling in love with Greyson, are you?"

"Of course not. What an idea!" I looked down at the little kitten. "You know he took Winston away from me. He has literally turned me out of there. If it weren't for Uncle Tom, I don't know where I'd be."

"If he's so keen on having Winston for himself, why doesn't he go back there?" Edmund said sensibly.

I shrugged. "Don't ask me. Perhaps he feels he should stay with me until Uncle gets here. I don't know."

"That's not likely," Edmund said slowly. "Greyson is up to something, I'm sure of it."

I looked at him in surprise. "What do you mean, Edmund? What could he be up to?"

Edmund appeared a little flustered. "Oh, just a feeling I have. I can't explain."

"It seems to me that Greyson has everything he wants right now." I stood up and walked over to the window. "He has Winston, and in the event of my uncle's death he would own the Plas, too."

"Perhaps not." Edmund looked down at his hands, and I couldn't see the expression in his eyes.

"Don't be exasperating, Edmund. Do you know something I do not?"

He shook his head. "I'm not at liberty to divulge any secrets, as well you know, Charlotte, but don't think everything is as simple as it looks on the surface."

I longed to shake the truth from him, but his lips were firmly closed, and I knew he would say no more on the subject.

It was great fun showing Edmund around the Plas. He took my arm, and we wound our way through the trees, coming suddenly into the clearing where the tiny chapel stood. Edmund drew a sharp breath and stood quite still.

"It is lovely, isn't it? Would you like to go inside?"

I went forward and opened the large carved doors, leading the way into the cool dimness. Fresh flowers stood on the altar, even though the winter weather had returned with a vengeance, and all the woodwork was fragrant with polish.

"Isn't it lovely, Edmund?" I looked around, but he seemed to be scrutinizing the floor boards. I went up behind him, curious about his actions.

"More interested in the architecture, are you?" I asked playfully.

"Look, these are loose," he said. "There must be a trap door here. Ah, yes, here's the handle."

He struggled a little, and the trap door opened, revealing a flight of dark stone steps.

"Shall we go and look?" Edmund glanced up at me eagerly, like a small boy discovering a secret hideaway.

I shrugged. "All right; whatever you say."

Lifting my skirts high, I followed him downward, shivering as the dank cold draught breathed its evil breath into my face.

There seemed to be numerous passages leading away from the central point of the staircase, and before I could stop him, Edmund had chosen his direction and was heading away into the darkness.

"Come back," I called, but my voice echoed emptily, thinning out into unnerving silence.

Tentatively I went forward a few steps, trying to peer through the gloom. We were foolish to have ventured down there without a lantern. For a moment I stood quite still, undecided whether to go after Edmund or to return to the chapel and let him find his own way back.

"Edmund!"

The sound of my own voice frightened me, and as I turned to climb back up the steps I heard a sound above me. Suddenly I was in complete darkness; someone had closed the trap door.

Bumping my knee hard in my haste, I scrambled up and began to thump on the wood of the floor boards. Surely whoever was up there could not fail to hear my cries.

After shouting and banging for about half an hour, I gave up any attempt to make myself heard and sat back on the coldness of the steps, wondering what to do next.

There seemed only one thing to do: go and look for Edmund. He might be hurt, or he might even have come out somewhere at the other end. That at least was a cheering thought, because then he would waste no time before bringing help to look for me.

Cautiously I went forward, putting one foot slowly in front of the other and feeling along the cold walls with my hands in the hope of discovering a doorway.

I don't know how long I walked thus, calling every now and again to Edmund, more to keep my spirits up than because I had any hope of finding him.

Suddenly, through the darkness, I heard a soft rustling sound as if someone were walking lightly toward me.

"Edmund?" I said hopefully. But there was no answer; just the soft movements coming nearer. "Who is it?" I said, my voice cracking with fear.

A hand touched mine. I screamed without realizing it was my own voice I heard, and then I was being drawn gently but surely forward.

Terrified, I could do nothing but follow, though the hand holding mine was gentle, with no hint of violence in its touch. Soon I felt fresh air, and the scent of the sea in my nostrils revived me, bringing back some of my wits.

"Who are you?" I asked through lips that trembled.

There was no answer to my question, but I felt

something metallic being put into my hand, and instinctively my fingers closed around the object. There was a gentle push, and before me I saw a tiny pinprick of light that indicated an opening.

"Thank you, whoever you are," I said, and hurried forward, feeling almost faint with relief.

Never had I been so glad to see the dark overcast winter clouds above my head. Behind me was the almost invisible entrance to the passages, and before me, only a few yards away, was the water of the estuary.

Breathlessly I scrambled up the rocks toward the edge of the gardens, breathing deeply of the cold salt air, thankful for the throbbing pain in my knee, which at least assured me that I was alive.

"Charlotte! Where on earth have you been?" Greyson, his dark hair ruffled, was hurrying toward me. His hands, warm and comforting, drew me over the low wall.

"Is Edmund all right?" I asked quickly, stopping to draw a breath.

"Yes, he came back here ages ago, saying something about you being down near the water with him. I was worried when you didn't return."

He still held my hands, and I was grateful for his support, making my shortness of breath an excuse for not answering him. Obviously, for some reason Edmund didn't want Greyson to know the truth about the passages. All the same, it would have been too bad for me if the mysterious stranger hadn't come along to show me the way out.

"The tides can be quite dangerous, you know, Charlotte," Greyson said reprovingly. "You are not used to the sea, so please use a little caution."

I nodded and stopped for a moment to look back down at the grey-green water, and for an instant thought I'd seen a flutter of black among the bushes; then I blinked, and there was nothing but the sea and the rocks.

"What on earth is this thing you're clutching in your hand?"

Greyson tried to uncurl my fingers, but obstinately I held on. Seeing the glint of a silver chain, I said the first thing that came into my head.

"Oh, my locket broke when I was climbing. Don't worry about it." I tried to smile, but I felt sick, and my legs still didn't have any strength in them.

"You are going straight to your room," Greyson said. "You look as though you'd seen a ghost."

Wenna fussed over me so much that, if I hadn't known better, I'd have said she was genuinely concerned.

"That's a nasty bruise you've got on your knee," she said, watching me as I examined it. "I'll bring you something to bathe it with right away."

When she was out of the room, I took the opportunity to look at the chain I was still clutching in my hand. At the end of it was a large oval locket, and inside there was a likeness of a man, a woman and a child. It told me nothing, and, disappointed, I slipped it around my neck. At least it proved to me that I wasn't going mad, and that down there in the darkness of the passages I'd actually made contact with someone.

Wenna came back presently, followed by one of the maids carrying a tray with a bowl and some bandages on it. Wenna herself was making me tea.

"It's good of you to go to all this trouble," I said.

"It's no trouble. Drink this, and you'll feel better."

As soon as the maid had left the room, Wenna came and sat beside me.

"Tell me, Charlotte, what really happened today?" She stared directly at me, and at once my guard was up.

"I don't know what you mean," I said quietly. "Edmund and I were exploring the grounds, and we lost sight of each other, that's all." I straightened my leg cautiously; it felt better already. "By the way, Wenna, Edmund is going to come and see me, isn't he?"

She shrugged her elegant shoulders and gestured with her tapering fingers.

"No one is preventing him. I don't think he is feeling very well himself."

Suddenly she was alert, her eyes widening as they looked at the locket hanging round my neck.

"Where did you get that?" she asked, her voice scarcely more than a whisper. All the color seemed to have left her face, and suddenly she looked almost old.

"Why, Wenna, is it something I shouldn't have?" I asked anxiously.

She made an obvious effort to pull herself together, though her hands were clenched at her sides, as if she were in pain.

"On the contrary, it is yours by right." I hardly heard her, she spoke so quietly.

"How is it mine by right? What do you mean?" I asked in bewilderment.

"It was your mother's," she said. "But it has been missing for years. You must tell me where you found it."

I really didn't know what to say. How could I tell the story of the stranger in the underground passage? It sounded stupid, even to myself.

I was saved from thinking up an answer by a knock on the door. To my relief, Edmund stood there, a smile on his face.

Wenna immediately got to her feet. "Excuse me," she said in her usual calm manner. "There are things I must attend to."

Edmund held the door for her to leave, and then

he bounded over to me, throwing the fluffy white kitten onto my lap.

"I found him crying outside," he said. "Now tell me what happened to you."

"You left me alone down there! That's what happened to me!" I said in mock anger.

"Oh, Charlie, I called and called. It was as if you'd disappeared from the face of the earth. I admit it was foolish of me to take you down there in the first place. I ought to have my head examined!" He picked up my hand and kissed it. "How did you get out, anyway?"

"Through the trap door, how else?" I said brightly, trying him out.

"Oh, Charlotte, how tame!" He flung his head back and laughed. "I might have known that you would take the easy way out, while I was down there like a mole in a hole."

"Why did you ask?" I said suspiciously. "Wasn't it the obvious thing for me to do when you went off and left me?"

He inclined his head. "Maybe; it just didn't seem like you to close the door on me," he said, puzzled.

I gave a sigh of utter relief. I'd been a fool to harbor even a hint of suspicion about Edmund.

It was only when he'd gone, closing the door quietly behind him, that I realized he'd never told me how he had gotten out of the passages.

CHAPTER SIX

Greyson seemed to go out of his way to be pleasant to me in the next few days, even going so far as to arrange a party for me to meet some of his friends.

Edmund decided to stay until after the party. "In that way I'll be able to celebrate Christmas twice," he said, smiling disarmingly at Greyson, who didn't respond with much enthusiasm.

We were all seated in the drawing room, and Wenna was making calculations in a notebook. Luxuriously I stretched my toes toward the fire, enjoying the air of festivity that seemed to have affected everyone in the household.

"That little kitten is very affectionate." Greyson leaned forward disturbing Fluffy, as I had named him, from his sleep. Tiny claws shot out and caught Greyson on the back of his hand.

"I don't think the animal likes you," Edmund commented, hardly able to conceal his amusement. "They are supposed to be good judges of people, aren't they?"

Greyson didn't bother to answer. He rose and poured himself a glass of wine, and I noticed Wenna was suddenly tense, her eyes never leaving Greyson's face.

"I'm sorry about that," I said soothingly. "You frightened him, that's all. Look, he loves to be smoothed, don't you, Fluffy?"

Greyson returned to my side, but ignored the kitten completely. There was a set look on his face, and I shuddered, realizing for the first time how formidable an enemy he could be.

"How many of the townspeople are coming to the party?" I asked quickly, and Wenna launched into an account of the guest list and discussed, mostly with Greyson, what meat should be provided for the main course.

"I'm looking forward to it," I said, trying to recapture my earlier feeling of warmth. "It's just what we all need to lighten the gloom of the winter."

Edmund was the first one to move away from the warmth of the fire and go to his room, and left alone with Greyson and Wenna, I felt an awkward third.

"Ah, well, early to bed and all that!" I said lightly, lifting the kitten up in my arms. "See you both in the morning."

Greyson followed me outside, his hand on my arm. "Don't worry about a gown, Charlotte," he said, smiling a little. "I have bought you one as a gift. I hope you like it."

"That's very kind of you, Greyson," I said, pleased at his thoughtfulness. "Very kind indeed."

"I've had it taken up to your room." His dark eyes glowed. "I'm sure you'll look very beautiful in it, Charlotte. A credit to the family."

Excitedly I hurried upstairs and into the bedroom. There, as Greyson had promised, was the dress spread over the bed. It was expensively cut of finest velvet, but as I held it against me, I wrinkled up my nose in disappointment. It was all black, with no relief of color anywhere.

For Wenna it would have been excellent, but against my pale skin it looked drab and unflattering. Still, I would have to wear it and make the best of it somehow. I couldn't bring myself to hurt Greyson's feelings.

Carefully I put the dress away.

Edmund was in his room, and I could find no one to relieve my boredom. At last, in desperation, I went into the library and picked a book at random from the shelves. It was in Welsh, but there was an inscription in the flyleaf in English which said simply "To my daughter, Charlotte."

Suddenly I heard movement behind me and spun round to see Greyson watching me.

"Getting ambitious, aren't you?" he said with a smile. "I should try that section over there; they are in English." He put his book down and came over to me, his hand resting lightly on my arm. "The gown, Charlotte—did you like it?" His eyes seemed to penetrate my very thoughts.

"It's a beautiful dress, Greyson, and you were very kind to think of me."

He seemed disappointed with my reply, and I realized he was too discerning to be easily put off.

"It's just a little somber as it is," I said quickly. "But I can easily remedy that." I smiled up at him. "Don't worry, Greyson. I'll try my best to do you credit."

"I know you will, Charlotte."

He leaned closer, and then his hand was warm on my cheek, and his lips brushed against mine. I stood quite still, my heart beating rapidly and my legs trembling. I was afraid to move lest I break the spell of the moment.

Greyson's arms encircled me and drew me closer, and suddenly I was standing on tiptoe, my arms around his neck. I had never felt like this before. I wanted the kiss to last forever, but he released me and went back to his chair near the fire.

"My dear Charlotte," he said a little shakily, "I've warned you before about waters that are too deep for you."

I stared at his back, feeling the tears come to my eyes. To him the moment had been nothing more than a game.

Without a word I turned and left the library, taking the stairs two at a time in a most undignified manner, so as to reach the privacy of my room more quickly.

I hated him, and I was a fool to let my heart rule my head.

Plas Melyn had been polished and cleaned until everything shone and sparkled like a new pin. Wenna was more relaxed now, knowing that all the preparations for the party were complete.

I had spent the entire afternoon trying to decide which way to decorate my dress to the best advantage, but for some reason nothing I did looked right, and eventually, I decided that I would just have to wear it as it was.

One of the maids had come to do my hair, and watching her nimble fingers as she fastened up the curls, I was reminded painfully of Jess. Not a very auspicious beginning for a party, I told myself sternly.

I could hear the sound of voices outside and knew that the guests were arriving. I would have to hurry. Greyson wanted me to be there to receive them.

My dress was laid out on the bed ready for me to slip into, and just as I was about to pick it up I noticed a long flat box resting against the velvet. I opened the lid and gasped in astonishment. Nestling inside on a soft white bed were the most exquisite emeralds I had ever seen. It was as if thousands of fires were alight inside the stones, and almost reverently, I picked them up and fastened them around my neck.

I noticed then that with the necklace was a pair of earrings—tiny stones, but equally beautiful. They swung from my ears and complemented the red lights of my hair beautifully, and as the maid fastened my dress, I saw that no other color would have done the stones justice.

Quickly I hurried downstairs just as Wenna was opening the doors and stood beside Greyson, feeling like a queen.

A host of people spoke to me, and I smiled without any effort, my heart warmed by the beautiful gift. I even had enough confidence to say a few words in Welsh, which Wenna had been teaching me, and a surprised spat of clapping greeted my little speech.

We sat at the large dining table that gleamed in the candlelight, and slowly I became aware that three people in the room were staring at me as if they'd never seen me before—Wenna, Greyson and Edmund.

I lifted my hand to them in a tiny wave, but without exception they ignored my gesture and stared fixedly at the gems around my throat.

I can't say that for me the evening was an outstanding success, even though all the eligible males paid me more than a fair share of attention. I could have been as ugly as sin, and no one would have noticed with those emeralds to look at.

It was with relief that I closed the door of my bedroom behind me and slipped out of the black dress, carefully replacing the blazing necklace and earrings on their cushion of velvet.

In my shift, I went and stood before the fire, taking comfort from its warmth and worrying about who had been the one to give me such valuable stones.

There was a pitiful sound from outside on the balcony, and for a moment my spine tingled with fear before I realized that somehow Fluffy had been shut outside. Smiling, I went and pulled back the curtain, turning the key in the lock and swinging the door open.

"Come on, puss," I said, hesitating as the coldness of the night air gusted in. The silly cat remained where he was, crying for attention, his small white back arched as he stood on the rail, waiting for me to carry him indoors.

With a sigh, I moved forward. But at the same time Fluffy changed his mind and took a flying leap, landing a few inches from my feet. He was poised for a moment, his bright eyes luminous as they stared at me, and then he was plunging downwards through the large hole that appeared suddenly in the boards. I screamed shrilly and stared at the terrace below, where I could just see the small still body.

I don't know who it was who took me inside and closed the door, or who pulled a blanket across my shoulders as I sat huddled on the bed. But a drink was thrust into my hands and, with tears streaming down my face, I obediently sipped the hot liquid.

"Come along, Charlotte; feet up, and I'll pull the clothes over you."

I think it was Wenna who coaxed me into bed, but I kept my eyes tightly shut, and soon a delicious feeling of weariness crept over me and I slept.

My mouth was dry when I awoke, and Greyson, sensing my discomfort, moved from my bedside and rang the bell.

"Charlotte, poor little Charlotte." He stared at me from across the room, and his expression was hard to read. "Misfortune seems to be dogging your footsteps very persistently."

"I struggled to sit up. "Someone is trying to kill me," I said flatly. "And last night they very nearly succeeded."

He returned to my bedside. "Have you any ideas about it? Did you see anyone at all lurking around your rooms?"

"Of course not," I said. "I would have mentioned

it, wouldn't I?"

Greyson shrugged. "You've been behaving so oddly, I don't really know what to think."

I stared at him. "I've been behaving oddly? That's rich, that is! Do you deny that it is only since my aunt died that attempts have been made on my life?" I frowned at him. "Come to think of it, as soon as you turned up on the scene."

"I've only your word for that," Greyson said calmly. "I never saw you in my life before. You could be an impostor, planted by someone in Aunt Grace's house."

I stared at him for a moment, my mouth open, the enormity of what he was saying taking a long time to sink in.

"That's stupid!" I said. "What about the servants? They knew me."

Greyson shook his head. "If you were an impostor, you would have paid people well to act as servants for you."

I was almost blustering in my indignation. "But am I trying to take my own life, then?"

Greyson stood up and smiled coolly down at me. "You must admit to having a remarkable number of lucky escapes, Charlotte dear. Not one of the attempts have been successful, has it?"

He didn't wait for an answer, which was just as well, because I was speechless with fury.

"And take those emeralds. They disappeared from the family many years ago, along with the locket that you now wear around your neck and which you lied to me about."

My hand went to the thin chain. It was still in place. I leaned back on the pillows and looked up at Greyson.

"Why are you so worried about my identity? Even if I was an impostor, there would be lean pickings for me now that you've taken Winston from me. What would I have here at the Plas? Uncle's charity. Would anyone be foolish enough to act a part for so little gain?"

"You almost make me believe you know nothing more," Greyson said, a glimmer of a smile in his eyes.

"What about your conduct, then? Is that what you would call normal?" I demanded, suddenly coldly angry. "First you turned up in the woods where I was attacked, and then when Jess was murdered, you pretended to be hurt when you were not!" I stared at him, but his expression didn't change. "William had you spotted for a fake straight away, and he heard one of the cutthroats saying you weren't to be harmed."

Greyson's eyebrows rose, and he tapped his boot as if considering what I'd just said.

"What about your friend Edmund?" he said suddenly. I looked at him in bewilderment, wondering at the change in the conversation.

"What about him?" I asked, wishing that I were miles away in the peace and quiet of the rolling hills and fields of Winston.

"Is the man the simpleton he appears, or is he after something?" He sat down astride a chair and crossed his arms, watching me closely.

"He wants to marry me, that's all," I said wearily. "So you see, Greyson, there is no need for me to play a part. I'd have more as Edmund's wife than I'd ever have as your cousin."

"Well, we'll leave it for now," he said, rising. "Oh, I nearly forgot. Your boy friend has gone off this morning without even saying goodbye. I wonder what cooled his ardor so quickly."

He threw a white envelope down on the sheets.

"He did leave you this," he added.

I unfolded the paper. It didn't take me long to read the few untidy lines Edmund had scrawled, telling me he thought it time that Uncle Tom were told of the events that were taking place at Plas Melyn. I looked up at Greyson, wondering if he had read it, and saw from the smile in his dark eyes that he had.

I bit my lip and crumpled the paper into a ball, throwing it in the direction of the fireplace. It fell short and landed on the floor at Greyson's feet. He kicked at it contemptuously and turned on his heel.

"I'd take things easy if I were you. Last night couldn't have been very pleasant for you, whoever planned it."

He went out, pulling the door quietly shut behind him, and I clenched my fists until my nails drew blood, longing to strike the smile from his handsome face.

I pulled on my cloak and left the house, my feet sinking into the crisp dry snow. The wind brought tears to my eyes, but I needed to be away from the atmosphere of suspicion that seemed to hang over the house.

I walked down to the water's edge, noticing with a sense of excitement that the tide was low, exposing a row of flat steppingstones that led out to the island.

Quickly, before I could feel afraid, I stepped out onto the first stone, and then there was no turning back. I knew I had to see the place for myself.

Rapidly I crossed the stones, which were treacherous under the light dusting of snow that still clung to them, and then I reached the island. Close to, it was flatter and longer than I'd first imagined. From the shore, it had looked like a mere hump in the water. The grass was spongy under my feet, but when I pressed forward the ground became hard, and here and there I could see the greyness of rock beneath the coarse grass.

It took only a few minutes for me to assure myself that there were no crosses, no mysterious open-
ings, and certainly nowhere a woman in a black dress
could suddenly appear from.

Well, at least I had looked; now I'd better get back
before the tide came in. The day, which had been
dull to start with, began to darken with clouds that
threatened still more snow. I stopped for a moment
to watch the progress of the clouds as they chased
rapidly across the sky, and from a long way off, I
thought I heard my name called.

There it was again—as faint as the cry of a bird,
but definitely my name! I turned to look at the shore
and was confused by the lighted windows from the
house that somehow made me feel very much alone.
Then I saw an arm waving frantically, beckoning me
back.

I hurried to the steppingstones and saw, to my
amazement, that the water was already swirling
around them, sucking noisily at the rocks as momen-
tarily the waves receded, only to return again even
more forcefully.

Quickly I stepped out and almost immediately lost
my footing, falling down hard on one knee. I didn't
pause to think about it. I pushed myself up from the
icy water and hurried on, feeling as though there
were a dragon at my back.

I couldn't blame anyone but myself, I thought rue-

fully as I fell at last onto the coldness of the shore
and lay for a moment in the snow, trying to get back
my breath. I looked toward the house, expecting to
see Wenna running down to where I lay, but the
gardens were empty.

I got to my feet and scrambled up the slope. One
thing was sure: the voice I'd heard calling was
Wenna's, and I knew I would have a lecture on my
foolhardiness. However, she didn't say a word. In
fact, she seemed surprised to see me in such a dis-
heveled state.

"Charlotte, what on earth have you been up to?"
she demanded, taking my soaking cloak away from
me.

I went to the fire and tried to warm some life back
into my numbed fingers.

"You know what I've been doing," I said impatiently. "You called me to warn me that the tide
was coming in quickly."

Her face was devoid of any expression. "What do
you mean?" she asked, shaking her head.

I sat down, my legs suddenly weak.

"Wenna, weren't you out there on the shore just
now, waving to me?"

"I haven't moved from this room, Charlotte," she
said faintly. She couldn't take her eyes from my
face, and I knew I must be as pale as she was.

"It *was* your voice," I said doggedly. "And then

when I looked up, I saw you waving to me."

She stood up so suddenly that her sewing box spilled out onto the floor. "I'll make you a cup of tea. You'll feel better with something warm inside you."

Her hands were shaking so much she could hardly hold the jug of water, and at last I rose and took it away from her, pushing her back into her chair.

"I'll do it," I said, suddenly filled with a calm I couldn't begin to understand. "And then, Wenna, you must tell me everything."

She covered her face with her hands, and I could tell by the shaking of her shoulders that she was crying.

I handed her the cup and seated myself opposite her, and after a few minutes she pulled herself together. She stretched her hand out and covered mine, her eyes large and luminous, staring at me oddly.

"You are not an impostor, are you, Charlotte?"

I was too surprised to answer. I just sat there, shaking my head.

"I feel it in my bones, and I've told Greyson that. He has to be careful, though, you see; so much responsibility."

"Wenna," I said gently, "you are not making sense."

The room was growing dark, and I wanted to move

away to light the candles. But she still held me in a strong grip.

"My sister," she said softly, "was your mother."

I suppose I should have been surprised, but strangely enough, I wasn't. I just sat looking at Wenna through the gloom, waiting for her to continue.

"I wanted to keep you here and bring you up, but it wasn't proper; you had to be brought up like a lady, because of your father's position. Then he died, just after your mother did. I don't think he could face life without her."

I was touched at the emotion in her voice, but I needed facts, concrete evidence to prove to myself who I was and what had been the circumstances of my birth.

"My mother," I said, "when she died, did she leave any letters? Any documents at all?"

I knew I was grasping at straws, but I desperately wanted to prove that my parents had been married. I wasn't willing to accept the stigma of illegitimacy.

"She didn't have time to leave anything," Wenna said simply. "She was drowned one day, out there on the island. There was nothing anyone could do."

She caught my hand more tightly. "She must be coming back to see you."

Wenna's voice was so matter-of-fact that she might have been discussing what meat we should have for our next meal. I tried to see her face, but the room was so dark now that only the glow from the fire relieved the gloom.

"What do you mean?" I was almost afraid to ask the question, though I almost expected what came next.

"That's why I'm sure you are no impostor," Wenna said gently. "The emeralds and the locket. They have been missing all these years, and yet now they turn up unexpectedly. It was she calling you from the shore. She didn't want history to repeat itself."

I jerked my hand away.

"I must light the candles," I said quickly.

The room came to life, and Wenna brushed back the strands of hair that were clinging to her face. I shivered, wondering what she'd say if I told her about the other things that had happened: my escape from the passages, and then the woman, dark hair blowing, standing out there on the island. The cross. The bobbing light. Was it possible I'd imagined it all?

Wenna was watching me. "You've seen her other times, haven't you?"

There was no point in denying it. "I've seen someone, I thought it was you." I drank my tea quickly, wondering if I was going mad.

Wenna was about to say more when the door swung open and Greyson breezed in, his cheeks flushed with the cold.

"What an atmosphere in here!" he exclaimed. "It's

as if someone had just died."

I shivered at his choice of words and looked at Wenna as if to protect her from hurt, but to my amazement, she was her usual serene self once more, her hair smooth and her hands still and tranquil against her dress.

"You'll need something hot, then." She smiled up at him, and he returned her smile, going to the fire and throwing more logs on it, stirring up a shower of sparks as he pushed the heel of his boot against the coals to move them.

I sat down and stared into my cup. My instinct to get away from the Plas had been a good one. Something very strange was happening there, and I felt that I wasn't going to come out of it too well.

"If you'll excuse me, I think I'll go to my room," I said quietly.

CHAPTER SEVEN

The next morning after breakfast, Greyson brought me my cloak.

"Put it on, Charlotte. I'm taking you for a drive." He smiled at me so charmingly that I immediately mistrusted his motives.

"Why do you intend to take me out?" I spoke more curtly than I'd meant to, but his expression didn't change.

"Dear Charlotte," he said, "you accept invitations so charmingly."

"What gives you the impression I'm accepting?" I asked, turning my back on him and walking into the drawing room.

He came after me. "Well, look, the sun is coming out and the snow has started to melt. Surely you would like to enjoy the countryside?"

I gazed through the window; the sun was gilding the water of the estuary so that it looked like gold.

"Drives with you into the country seem not with-out their dangers," I said, and shivered, as I could see again in my mind's eye Jess in my green velvet, dead on the road.

"Look upon it as a challenge," Greyson said. "I am going to see some old friends of Father's. They remember the family well—all the family."

I couldn't fail to see the significance of his words, and I turned to look at him.

"You think they'd recognize me from when I was a baby? They would have to have extraordinary powers of memory for that."

"Are you coming or not?" Greyson said, his eyes watching my every move.

"I'll come," I said quickly. "I may learn something to my advantage."

"Such as what?" Greyson asked coolly.

I took my cloak from his hand and walked past him.

"If we don't start soon, it will be too late to travel anywhere," I said, and led the way out into the yard, where the coach was waiting.

For some reason, Greyson chose to sit next to me. We seemed isolated from the rest of the world, and I felt a lift of my heart as his hand accidentally brushed against mine.

"It's a great pity," he said, half turning to look at me.

I looked away from him through the window to where the mountains rose above the road in sparkling white splendor.

"What is a pity?" I asked, though somehow I already knew what he was going to say.

"That we should have met in these circumstances." He took my hand deliberately, and his fingers were gentle and firm. "I think I could easily fall in love with you, Charlotte." His voice was soft, and I was acutely aware of his nearness.

"Is that your idea of a compliment?" I tried to sound angry, but my voice would hardly function.

"What are you, Charlotte—innocent or merely a victim of circumstances? That's what I'd like to know."

I drew my hand away impatiently. "If only I knew what you were talking about!" I felt the hot color rise to my cheeks. "What should I be guilty of? Please let me into the secret."

He sighed, but didn't move away, though I tried to get right into the corner of the seat. My heart was beating hard, and tears burned behind my lids.

"It will be all right if old Mrs. Grifiths can tell me that you really are Charlotte; then I'll confide in you. I'll tell you everything I know myself."

"How can she prove anything?" I asked, bewildered. "I've lived in Winston with Aunt Grace for as long as I can remember."

He took my fingers in his once more. "She'll know," he said, "and until then, we might just as well enjoy our day out. Don't you agree?"

"I agree," I said ruefully. "I don't see there's much else I can do!"

The coach jerked to a halt, and the horses pawed the ground, scenting water.

"Here, let me help you down. I think you will like eating in this tavern. It is reputed to be several hundred years old."

We went inside; across the roof stretched great thick beams of wood darkened by smoke and age. The walls were of thick rough stone, and a glowing fire filled the enormous hearth.

"It's lovely!" I said, and meant it.

I was hungry, and the chicken pie had a warm mouth-watering crust that melted between the teeth. Greyson smiled encouragingly, and I couldn't resist a jibe.

"Fattening me for the kill, is that it?" I drank some wine and found that my head was spinning.

"You'd better not drink too much of that stuff," Greyson said, smiling in a strangely carefree manner. "It's very potent and goes straight to your head."

"Now he tells me!" I laughed up at him, well aware that I was flirting. But it didn't seem to matter any more. Nothing mattered any more, come to that. "Who cares who or what I really am, anyway? If

I'm not here, does anyone stand to gain? No, of course not!"

I answered my own question, and Greyson's eyes were suddenly serious.

"No one wants me," I said, widening my eyes in mock tragedy. "No, I'm not wanted by anyone at all."

I looked at Greyson, and his face seemed to blur before my eyes.

"Charlotte, I think I'd better take you outside into the fresh air," he said, and caught my arm and led me out to the yard.

"People say they want me," I continued. "Uncle Tom says he wants me, but that's just because I'll be company for him when you go to live at Winston. And Edmund tells me he wants me to be his wife, but I think he depends on me. He has ever since I beat him at running, when we were children." I laughed a little hysterically. "The most unwanted person in the world, that's what I am."

I fell crying against Greyson's shoulder, and his hands were gentle as he brushed away my tangled hair.

"Come on; back to the coach. We are nearly there."

He had almost to lift me inside, and then I slumped back against the cushions and promptly fell asleep.

I became aware that something was banging insistently, and, startled, I sat up, straightening my dress around my ankles. Sleepily I looked out of the coach window to see Greyson knocking on the door of the tiny cottage. He disappeared around the back, and quickly stepped down into the hard, rough road.

"Greyson, what is it?" I shouted, and my voice was carried away by the wind.

He was leaning against the small window, and when I peered under his arm, I could see an overturned chair and pieces of broken crockery scattered over the floor.

"What's wrong?" I said in a whisper.

Greyson turned on me, his eyes blazing and his arm uplifted as if he would strike me. I think I screamed and crouched back against the wall, and slowly he lowered his hand to his side.

"Someone has gotten here first, to make sure she wouldn't talk," he said, and the bitterness in his voice was like a knife turning inside me.

"Greyson—" I touched his arm, but he pulled away as if I were poison. "Greyson, I didn't even know where we were going until this morning, and you've been with me all the time. How could I be involved in this?"

He didn't appear to hear me, but walked away, and I had the feeling that if I didn't hurry, he would leave me there alone on the barren hillside.

We spent the entire journey back sitting in silence,

and I could almost feel the anger that was burning him up. I didn't understand any of it, and furthermore, I wasn't going to try. After this, I would have to leave. It was obvious that Greyson and I couldn't remain together in the same house.

He didn't help me from the coach. He walked away from me, his face set, and slowly I followed him, feeling more tired and despondent than ever in my life before.

Wenna came into the hall and put her arm around me.

"Come up to bed, Charlotte. I'll bring you something on a tray," she said softly, and I could see that even she was frightened by the mood Greyson was in.

"Don't worry, Wenna," I said. "I'm not hungry. But I'd like a drink; my throat is dry."

When I was tucked into the sheets, Wenna held a cup to my lips, and gratefully I drank the hot tea. When I'd finished it there was a bitter taste in my mouth, and Wenna smiled reassuringly.

"You'll have a good sleep now, little one," she said.

Voices seemed to float above my head, and I lay quite still for a moment, trying to get my bearings. The bright sunlight struck against my eyelids, and suddenly a feeling of nausea almost overwhelmed me.

I sat up, aware that someone had just left the room, and I was angry that I was allowed no privacy in Plas Melyn.

Carefully I put my feet over the edge of the bed, and the room seemed to swing around me in large circles. I closed my eyes, but that only made it worse, and I forced myself to my feet and across to the bell.

Wenna brought me a tray of tea. I drank the steaming fragrant liquid, and after a few minutes the room returned to normal and I could sit up without feeling I was going to faint.

"You look awful this morning," Wenna said bluntly. "Why don't you stay in bed for a while?"

"I think I will."

Wearily I lay back against the pillows. One thing was certain: I couldn't face Greyson this morning.

I slept a little and awoke feeling slightly better, but when I got out of bed, my legs were still weak and trembling. One of the maids brought in fuel for the fire, and I asked her for warm water so that I could bathe my face. I don't think she understood me until I went through the pantomime of washing; then she smiled and nodded her head.

After I'd dressed I sat near the fire, wondering what I should do next. Should I write to Edmund and ask him to come and take me home? The thought was very tempting, but I wasn't sure that I wanted to spend my life with him. I suppose Greyson had made him seem just a little dim-witted and dull. I pushed the disloyal thought away quickly and went to the window. Perhaps a little fresh air would clear my mind.

I pulled aside the curtains that covered the glass door and, to my amazement, saw that bars had been placed over it. I peered out and saw with a shudder that the gaping hole in the floor boards hadn't been repaired. I sighed. No doubt the bars there merely as a protection, but I had the unpleasant feeling that I was a prisoner.

Later, when Wenna brought me some food, I managed to eat a little, though the feeling of nausea still persisted to some extent.

"I must leave here, Wenna," I said desperately. "I just can't live in such an atmosphere any longer."

Wenna sat down beside me. "Don't talk of leaving, not yet a while."

She was almost pleading with me. I looked at her in surprise. Since the day when she'd talked to me about my mother, she had reverted to her usual serene aloof self and had paid me only as much attention as was necessary. In fact, I had begun to doubt that the conversation had ever taken place at all.

"Have patience, Charlotte. Everything will turn out for the best, you'll see. Greyson is upset at the moment, but he'll understand everything one day."

I had no idea what she was talking about, but I

was too tired to argue.

"Soon," I said softly. "I'll have to go soon."

Suddenly I felt sleepy again, and my eyelids were too heavy to keep open. Wenna was leading me to the bed and tucking the clothes around me as if I were a child, talking to me soothingly in Welsh, and I relaxed and slept.

There was a loud knocking on the door, and before I could wake properly, Greyson was standing at the foot of the bed.

"What is wrong with you, Charlotte?" he said, his face angry and empty of any warmth.

"I don't know what's wrong," I said, feeling as if I were swimming through a bowl of honey.

He stared at me for a long time, then came and took my hand. "My God, Charlotte, you are painfully thin. I think I'd better get a doctor for you."

I struggled to sit up. "All I want to do is go home." I began to cry. "Please, Greyson, let me go to Winston for a few weeks. What harm can it possibly do?"

After agonizing moments of indecision, he nodded. "All right, as you are so set on it; and you really do look ill." He came and sat beside me and sighed heavily. He looked so boyish and worried, with his dark hair ruffled, I had the strangest feeling that I wanted to protect him.

"Something is very wrong here, Greyson," I said. "You must find out what it is before it is too late."

He stared at me for a moment, then put his arms round me and held me close. For a moment neither of us spoke, and I think he was almost as surprised by his action as I was. Slowly I reached up and touched his thick dark hair, and he pressed his cheek against mine and held me for several moments.

"I think I've fallen in love with you, Charlotte, but the terrible thing is, I don't trust you."

I withdrew gently from his arms. "I know you don't, but I can't help that, Greyson. And I don't even know what it is you suspect me of."

He stood up and crossed the room, his eyes closed wearily as he stood before the fire. The only sound in the room was the fall of the logs in the grate as he considered what I had said.

"All right." He spoke so suddenly that I jumped. "I'll take you back to Winston. It's obvious to me that you are ill, and I can't watch you growing worse, that's certain." He smiled ruefully. "I'll make arrangements immediately, and we'll see what a few weeks in your old home will do for you."

Tears of joy came to my eyes, and impatiently I brushed them aside. I was going home; what more could I ask?

There was a knock on the door, and Wenna let herself in, glancing anxiously at me as she went to stand beside Greyson.

"How is she?" she asked quietly.

Greyson looked down at her and smiled. "Charlotte feels better already. I've promised to take her home."

For a moment I thought Wenna would faint, and then somehow she pulled herself together.

"Well, in that case I'd better see to everything," she said smoothly. And with her head high, she left the room.

Greyson grimaced. "I don't think she wants you to leave," he said. "She doesn't think you are well enough to travel. Perhaps she's right."

"No!" I said. "If I don't go now, I've the feeling I'll never see Winston again."

He laughed. "A bit dramatic, my dear Charlotte." He sat near the bed once more and took my hand.

"Greyson, will you take me out somewhere, please? I feel I must have some fresh air."

He looked at me doubtfully. "I don't know if that's wise. I'm sure Wenna wouldn't like it."

"Never mind Wenna. *I'm* asking you, and I remember saying I'd never ask you for any favors again, so you can see how much it means to me. I must get out of the Plas for an hour or two."

"All right. Get your things, and I'll take you into Graig Melyn. Perhaps a change of scenery will do you good."

As the coach rocked along the sea road, I breathed in the clean salty air, and at last my head began to clear. By the time we had walked through the gardens and looked into the shop windows, I felt ravenously hungry.

"Come with me." Greyson smiled. "I know where we can get the crispest bread and the most mellow cheese in the whole of Wales. And afterwards we'll have the creamiest cake we can find. "I'll fatten you up!"

Laughing like children, we hurried through the streets, and as the sun shone warmly on my back, I wished the day could last forever.

"Charlotte, are you awake?" It was Wenna, and I glanced down at the cold tea in my cup and hastily tipped it into the plant bowl; then I lay on the bed and turned my face to the wall, pretending to sleep.

"Poor little mite." Wenna was obviously standing over me. "I wish I could help you to be with your loved ones more quickly. Poor little Charlotte."

She bent down and pulled a shawl over my shoulders, and her hands were gentle. How could I even suspect her of doing me harm? All the same, I kept quite still and listened as she moved around the room, opening cupboards and moving my possessions about.

Perhaps she was packing my clothes for me. I turned over onto my back. Hearing the movement, she glided over the floor and let herself out quietly.

I went to the cupboard and looked inside. There among my dresses was a box, and around it Wenna had tied some bright ribbons. Curiously I opened it and gasped in astonishment. Inside the box was the most beautiful gold and sapphire pendant I had ever seen. I picked it up and held it to the light, and a thousand candles might have been glowing behind the large stones.

There was a knock on the door, and quickly I hid the pendant behind my back.

"Oh, you are awake now. Wenna told me to call you for tea," Greyson said as he came into the room, looking at me anxiously. "Is anything wrong, Charlotte? You look quite pale. I hope you are not feeling ill again. I had hoped you were improving."

"Look at this, Greyson. Wenna just put it in my cupboard." I held the gleaming trinket out, he came and took it from me.

"Are you sure?" he said in bewilderment. "Wenna has never owned anything as valuable as this, not to my knowledge, anyway."

"Of course I'm sure," I snapped impatiently. "I saw her put the box in my cupboard."

"Why didn't she give you the box directly?" Greyson sat down on the bed and examined the pendant closely.

For a moment I didn't know how to answer. How could I tell him I had been feigning sleep?

"I was half asleep, and I saw her put the box in the cupboard," I said. "I suppose she didn't want to wake me."

Greyson looked at me. "If you were half asleep, then you couldn't be sure it was Wenna."

I shrugged. "Of course it was Wenna. I heard her voice." As soon as I spoke, I realized how silly I sounded.

"Whom was she speaking to, if you were half asleep?" Greyson said quickly, and I had the feeling I was being cross-examined for some reason that I didn't understand.

"Why all this," I said, "just because Wenna left me a present? I wish I hadn't shown you now."

He threw the pendant at me. "There is an inscription that should interest you," he said. "That was one of the pieces of jewelry given to your mother from the Plas Melyn estate. Its rumored that there's a great deal more of it hidden around the Plas, worth an awful lot of money."

I stared at him. "I see. And that's what you think I'm after, is it? You are afraid I might be entitled to my mother's belongings, and you want them for yourself!"

He flushed a dull red. "They haven't even been proved to exist yet, but if they do, I intend to make sure the right person gets them."

"It is obvious they exist." I went to the cupboard and brought out the emeralds; then I slipped the locket from my neck. "There is some of it; and you are welcome to it and to anything else that turns up. All I want to do is get away from here—as far away as possible!"

I sat down and began to cry, and after a while Greyson gently placed the jewels in my hands.

"Take them," he said softly. "They will buy you a home as lovely as Winston, and more."

I looked up at him hopefully. "Then you won't consider letting me have Winston and keeping them for yourself? Look how much you could do to the Plas with all that money."

He shook his head. "You mustn't push your luck, Charlotte. Won't you ever learn that?"

CHAPTER EIGHT

For a few days Greyson avoided me, but at last I managed to track him down in the library. He was sitting quietly in the firelight, his feet stretched out before him.

"I must speak to you," I said quietly. "It's about me going to Winston. You did agree, didn't you?"

"Sit down, Charlotte," he said, and his voice was filled with sadness.

Reluctantly I sat beside him, waiting for him to tell me what was wrong.

"It's my father," he said at last. "He's very ill."

He sighed and stirred the fire so that it flared for a moment, revealing his face, strained with worry and looking even thinner than usual.

"Poor Uncle Tom," I said. "I'm sorry, Greyson."

"He's coming home," he said. "The journey will probably do him more harm than good, but he wants to be here." He looked at me. "You should understand the feeling, Charlotte; you love Winston so much."

I bent my head, fiddling with the embroidery on my skirt and not knowing what to say.

"You can go back to Winston, of course," Greyson said slowly, "but I'd appreciate it if you would stay here for a while. My father sets such store by you."

Disappointment hung like a stone around my neck, but how could I refuse such a request?

"I'll stay as long as Uncle Tom needs me," I said quietly. "When will he arrive?"

Greyson moved a little in his chair. "Sometime to-morrow, I think. William will travel with him. I'm sure he'll look after him very well."

"Yes, of course he will."

The hot color came to my cheeks as I remembered confronting Greyson with Will's suspicions about him, but Greyson didn't seem to notice.

"I've come to a decision," he said suddenly. "You can have Winston. I'll make the deeds over to you."

I stared at him in surprise. "But what about all the talk of me being an impostor? Surely you couldn't give the house over to someone who isn't entitled to it?"

He waved his hand in the air. "I don't think it really matters any more," he said, and leaned his head back wearily against the cushions.

It was only later, when I sat alone in my room,

that I understood the reason for Greyson's generosity. Once my uncle died, he would be the sole owner of Plas Melyn and anything that might be found on the grounds. I would be shut up with the gift of Winston and would be neatly out of his way.

In the morning Wenna knocked, and I jumped out of bed quickly to open the door for her. She wasted her effort every day by bringing me up a tray, because I never drank the tea now for fear it might be poisoned.

As I climbed over my dress that had fallen to the floor, I noticed something shining in its folds. Icy fingers tingled down my spine as I realized that it was another piece of jewelry.

"How on earth did that get here?" I whispered, and hurried around the room, checking the window catches. Then, as Wenna banged impatiently, I went to the door. It was locked, the key still in place.

I swung the door open and returned to the bed, deliberately not looking at my dress in a heap on the floor.

Wenna handed me the tray. "It's a lovely day, Charlotte. You should try to get out for a walk. It will put some color into those pale cheeks of yours."

Before I could stop her, she bent down and picked up my dress.

"Untidy child!" she reproved me, smiling, and then stared in fascination as a gleaming diamond brooch fell onto the carpet. "It's lovely!" she said softly. "Your mother has been to see you again. No, don't say anything at all." Reverently she placed the brooch beside me on the bed.

"How could anyone get in here?" I said in horror. "Are they any spare keys, do you know?"

Wenna shook her head. "Your mother wouldn't need a key, child. Come now, don't be upset. She wants you to be happy."

I managed to pull myself together. "Thank you, Wenna; you are right, of course. There's no need to get upset."

I watched as she went out, then took the tea and threw it out of the window as far as it would go.

"She's mad! I don't believe in spirits, especially ones who bring gifts like this," I said aloud.

Defiantly I wore the brooch down to breakfast and saw with triumph how Greyson's eyes rested in amazement on the flashing stones.

"Another gift," I said abruptly. "It came in the night, even though my door and windows were locked. Do you believe in the supernatural, Greyson?"

He looked at me through tired eyes, and I was sorry for the hostility in my voice.

"There must be some logical explanation," he said quietly, and the words were like an accusation.

"Well, one thing is certain," I said sarcastically. "You only have to wait a little while, and the family heirlooms will all be returned to you. I'll trade them gladly for the deeds to Winston."

He stared at me with distaste. "Keep them all, if you like. You are certainly putting on a convincing performance."

Wenna bustled in and placed some fresh tea on the table.

"Come along now, you two; you are not quarreling, surely?" she said brightly, though her eyes missed nothing.

"Why should we quarrel?" Greyson said quietly. "So long as Charlotte gets what she wants, she is quite amenable."

I rose and left the table, my color high and my hands shaking. Obviously, the sight of the brooch had convinced my cousin that I was a fortune hunter who had somehow found the key to the missing riches.

He came up to my room later and checked the windows, then tested the lock on the door.

"No one could possibly have gotten in," he said. "Could the brooch have been planted here last night?"

I shook my head. "I've thought of that. I took my dress off after I'd locked the door and windows, and there was certainly no brooch then."

Greyson sat down and looked thoughtfully around, his sharp eyes searching the walls.

"There could, of course, be a concealed doorway," he said thoughtfully.

"The passages!" I said excitedly. "It's just possible that some of them cross to the house."

Greyson leaned against the wall and looked at me. He crossed his arms and waited for an explanation.

"One day Edmund found a trap door in the chapel. Surely you knew it was there?" I looked at Greyson incredulously as he shook his head. "Well, down beneath it, there were passages leading off in all directions. I got shut down there."

I stopped, not knowing how to tell him that a strange unknown person had taken my hand and led me to a way out.

"And Edmund?" Greyson asked, his eyebrows raised.

I smoothed down the skirt of my dress and frowned. "He got out somehow. I forgot to ask him about it."

I looked up and saw that Greyson was considering what I had said. His eyes met mine in a long look.

"Well, well, it seems as though I've underestimated good old Edmund," he said. "He wants to marry you, doesn't he?" He came and sat beside me.

I nodded. "I've never made any secret of it, and neither has he. It's probably what Aunt Grace wanted."

Greyson shook his head. "No, that's not what Aunt Grace wanted at all, Charlotte."

"How on earth do you know that?" I said angrily. "I lived with her, remember?"

He smiled. "But I was her heir; and along with her papers was a letter for me. She wanted you to marry me."

Unaccountably, my heart was beating faster. I lowered my eyes, trying to turn away from his penetrating gaze.

"Why would she want that?" I asked in a muffled voice.

"Why indeed?" he said, and the amusement in his voice was apparent as he continued to stare at me.

Suddenly his lips were close to mine. He turned my face with his hand, and I no longer wished to struggle. I closed my eyes, waiting breathlessly.

His kiss was so light, I hardly felt it. He moved away and disappointed, I looked up at him.

"There is really no need to play fast and loose with my affections." My voice shook in spite of myself, and I flounced angrily past him. "I'm going out!" I said. "And when I come back, I don't want to see you in my room!"

He shrugged mockingly. "I was only trying to help, but go on out if you want to. I'm not going to stop you."

I ran down the stairs and out into the fresh spring breeze. Somewhere behind me I heard a voice calling, but I took no notice.

I followed the road leading in the opposite direction from Graig Melyn. I didn't want anyone from the town to see me like this. I'd gone only a few hundred yards when I heard someone running behind me. I turned to see Greyson, a grin on his face and his dark hair driven all over the place by the breeze.

"Charlotte, you must be cold!" he called, and caught up with me, gasping for breath.

"Not a bit!" I said, staring straight ahead.

He fell into step behind me.

"What a shame. I seem to have brought my cloak with me for nothing, then," he said, and burst out laughing.

"Oh, give it here!"

I snatched it out of his hands and wrapped it around my shoulders, thankful for its warmth.

"Where are we going?" he asked, and his voice had a cheerful ring to it such as I hadn't heard in a long time.

"I'm going for a walk," I said haughtily.

He caught up with me easily and put his arm around my shoulder, drawing me in closer to protect me from the breeze.

"We'll just forget all our troubles and enjoy our walk, shall we?" he said softly, and I closed my eyes for a moment, drinking in the softness of the air and the drowsy scents that drifted from the mountain flowers.

"It would be wonderful if things could always be this peaceful and uncomplicated." I breathed deeply.

"I feel I could walk for miles."

"Well, let us do just that!" Greyson smiled down at me in a challenge. "We'll walk until we get tired and then find a place to eat. There are plenty of inns along this road. Then when we've had enough, we can turn around and go back again."

"Why not?" I laughed for the sheer joy of being in his company when he was in such a happy mood.

Although we kept the conversation light, there was an instant feeling of communication between us; it was almost as if we could read each other's thoughts before they were spoken. We found a great deal to laugh at, and by the time we found an inn, I was completely relaxed and very hungry.

It was called The Crow's Nest, not surprisingly, as it hung precariously on the side of the mountain, looking as if the lightest of showers would dislodge it.

I sat down thankfully and stretched my feet out toward the bright fire which, even on a warm spring day, was a necessity because of the way the wind whistled around the walls. The smiling landlord attended to us immediately, and soon I was ravenously eating a whole chicken and ham pie.

"I'm glad to see you are better now, Charlotte," Greyson said in all seriousness. "Several weeks ago you weren't eating enough to keep a bird alive."

A cloud dimmed my happiness as I thought of

the countless cups of tea I'd thrown away. If I'd been drinking them, I'd have been dead by now, I was convinced.

Aware of my change of mood, Greyson leaned forward. "What's wrong, Charlotte? Have I said something to upset you?"

For a moment, I was tempted to tell him everything, but some sense of caution halted me. How did I know that it wasn't Greyson himself who had been administering the poison?

"Oh, no, nothing's wrong. I'm just more tired than I thought, I suppose."

"Come along then; we'll start back and take it slowly. I'm a fool to have let you do too much."

With his arm around me, how could I believe him capable of murder? I leaned against him, my eyes closed, feeling the sun strike warmly against my cheeks. I loved him achingly, and yet I hardly knew what to believe.

Suddenly he let me go, and I opened my eyes wide in astonishment to see him run along the road after a small pony and trap.

I hurried as best I could, tripping over the stones and bits of shrubbery that jutted out all over the place, and saw to my horror that Greyson was attempting to leap onto the back of the cart. I held my breath until I saw his legs swing up and over, and then he had a good footing. He brought the pony to a halt and looked back, waving to me to join him.

I was breathless when he almost lifted me off the ground and deposited me on the wooden seat.

"Charlotte, I want you to meet an old friend of mine," he said, and I glanced sharply at the elderly lady covered with a shawl who sat limply holding the reins in her gnarled hands. "I hope you don't mind, but we are going visiting," Greyson said, and took over the handling of the pony, flicking him lightly so that he broke into a brisk trot down the uneven track.

I was bewildered, but Greyson seemed so angry that I was afraid to question him. I just sat where I was and waited to see what would happen.

We stopped eventually outside an old cottage, and at once I recognized it as the one he'd brought me to, to meet Mrs. Grifiths.

"Here we are." Greyson helped me down and then turned to the old lady. "Come along, Mrs. Grifiths; I think you've got some explaining to do."

Inside the cottage everything gleamed, a far different picture from the one we'd seen when we'd looked through the window before.

"Was it money?" Greyson asked bluntly, and the old lady sank down into a chair, nodding her head.

"Greyson, will you explain what's going on?" I said, watching in amazement as he replenished the fire and placed a kettle of water on it as if every inch of the room were familiar to him.

"I told you that the Grifiths family were old friends, didn't I?" he said quietly. "And before you were taken to England, you were left for a few months in this lady's capable hands. That's why I knew she could identify the real Charlotte."

"But why didn't Wenna look after me?" I said. "She wanted to!"

I sat down on the small stool of polished oak, holding my hands toward the fire.

"She was ill," Greyson said briefly, and went to stand before the old lady. "I was only about eight years old myself, but Father used to bring me here often. We had quite a lot of money in those days, and I don't think Mrs. Grifiths ever suffered from a lack of generosity on the part of my father, or yours, when he was alive."

Mrs. Grifiths looked down at her hands; so far she hadn't spoken a word.

Greyson crouched on his heels before her. "Why did you frighten me like this? And who was it who paid you?"

She shook her head and stared at him as if he had a viper hidden inside his coat.

"Go away. Leave decent folks alone!" she said sharply, and there was something in the way she glanced at the door behind her that brought prickles to my spine.

I don't know if my nerves were alert, or if my imagination was playing tricks on me, but I thought I heard a noise in the distant room.

"Come along, Greyson. Leave Mrs. Grifiths to rest. Perhaps we can call on her another day."

I tried to signal to him with my eyes, and he seemed to know there was a reason for my words.

"We'll take your pony and trap, if you don't mind," he said, and got to his feet, dropping some money onto the table. "You'll have it back first thing in the morning, don't worry."

With an angry gesture, she pushed the coins onto the floor.

"Take it back!" she said. "There are some things more important than money."

I was relieved that we didn't have to walk all the way back to the Plas. Dusk was falling over the mountain tops and creeping across the valley like a dark lace shawl.

"Well, what did you make of that, Charlotte?" Greyson asked, and for once he seemed at a loss.

"She's got someone in that house, I'm pretty—someone she's afraid of."

"Why do you say that?" Greyson asked in surprise, glancing back over his shoulder to where the cottage nestled among the trees.

"A feeling mostly, but I think I heard a movement in the other room. Didn't you see the way she looked at the door?"

Greyson was silent. I could hear the wind whipping around us like the cry of a hundred birds. I shivered and huddled closer against his shoulder.

"I'm frightened," I said suddenly. "I can't explain it, but I feel we are not alone out here."

"Don't worry, Charlotte; you are safe with me," he said. And as the moon began to slide out like a pale moth against the sky, I saw him smile down at me reassuringly.

To my relief, I finally saw the lights of Plas Melyn appear like fireflies along the coastline.

"Wenna will be worried," Greyson said. "She's put candles in every window, I'd say, wouldn't you?"

"Look!" I said, grasping his arm. "There on the island. Someone is there with a lamp."

Unmistakably, there was a light, and the stark arms of a cross rose against the silver sky.

"Yes, I see it," Greyson said. "What on earth would anyone be doing out there now? And with a cross?"

"Thank God I'm not seeing things!" I was so relieved I could hardly get the words out. "I was beginning to think I was going mad."

The island was hidden from us for some of the way as the road cut deeply into the mountainside. Then we were drawing nearer to the Plas, and as Greyson clucked his tongue to stop the pony, I saw that there was nothing out there but the sea and the little hump of land.

Greyson stood beside me, his arm around my shoulder. "It seems we are having visions, my dear Charlotte, except that I, for one, don't believe in them."

Wenna was almost hysterical when we went inside. She rushed toward us and fussed around as if we were tiny children who had been lost in the darkness.

"Come into the kitchen, and I'll make you something hot," she said. Her hands were shaking so much that she was forced to clutch the dark material of her dress to control them.

"Don't worry," Greyson said easily. "You go to bed, Wenna. Charlotte and I will find something for ourselves."

I turned to say something to her, but there was such a look of hatred in her eyes that it took my breath away. Without another word, she left us, and I followed Greyson into the kitchen, feeling as though I'd been condemned to death.

CHAPTER NINE

I had almost decided to walk down to the beach when it began to rain. Large dots of moisture spread themselves on the windowpanes as if trying to get into the warmth of the room.

"Not thinking of going out, are you?" Greyson asked as he walked past me, dressed in his big coat.

"No, I'm not now," I said. "But you obviously intend to." I walked with him to the door, breathing in the chill night air.

"I'm going over to the chapel," Greyson said. "I don't want anyone to know I'm there, so don't say a word."

"But, Greyson," I said urgently, "it could be dangerous, especially if you don't know the passages."

"Don't worry about me," he said. "If you can find your way around, I'm sure I can. I know the lay of the land, for one thing."

"Leave it till morning, at least," I suggested. But he was gone, striding through the darkness.

I shrugged and closed the door. He was big enough to take care of himself, and anyway, what did he have to fear? I went into the library, chiding myself for my foolishness. But just the same, I couldn't help being uneasy.

By chance, I took down the same book as before and stared at my name written on the yellow page.

"My poor father," I said aloud, and then laughed at myself and sat before the fire, the book in my lap.

A thought suddenly occurred to me. No doubt my father had imagined I would grow up at the Plas; otherwise why had he left a book with my name on it? Yet he must have known his brother would have his estate. I shrugged. What was one book, anyway?

I leafed through the pages, and most of the words meant nothing to me. Unfortunately, my lessons in Welsh seemed to have come to an end.

A single word was scrawled on the back pages, filling both sides of the book. I couldn't understand it, but there seemed to be an angry ring to it.

" 'Bradwr,' " I said softly. "Now what does 'Bradwr' mean?"

I should have to ask Wenna, if I could catch her in a good mood. I leaned back in the chair and closed my eyes. It was peaceful in the library, and the rain rattling in earnest against the windows made me glad of the warm fire.

I must have dozed a little, because when I opened

my eyes again the candles had burned down and the
fire was low in the grate. I sat up, shivering, and
wondered if Greyson had returned. It was silly of me
to worry about him, but somehow I couldn't help
myself.

I looked into the kitchen, and it was silent and
empty. It seemed larger than usual in the darkness,
and, shuddering, I closed the door.

There was no one in the drawing room, either,
and I came to the conclusion it must be very late
and everyone was in bed.

Carefully I made my way up the darkened staircase and fumbled for the door of my room. Luckily,
the fire was still glowing, and I quickly lit the candles,
breathing a sigh of relief as the darkness was dis-
pelled.

I didn't know what to do. I could hardly march
into Greyson's room; and yet I couldn't think of
sleeping while I was still not certain if he had returned or not.

I sat on the bed and kicked off my shoes, leaning
wearily against the pillows. I felt uneasy somehow,
as if day had turned into night while I wasn't looking.

I rubbed my eyes, wondering if I'd caught a cold
in them; they seemed to be burning and irritated
in a most uncomfortable way. Come to think of it,
there was a peculiar smell in the room, too, almost

as if something were burning.

I started to cough and then got to my feet, making my way to the mantelpiece where I'd stood the candlesticks. I remember reaching out toward them to extinguish the strange flame, and then I was dropping down into a pool of darkness that seemed to have no bottom. . . .

It might have been only minutes later that I opened my eyes, but it could have been longer. I was lying stretched across the carpet, with an empty holder clutched in my hand.

I tried to sit up, and then I became suffocatingly aware of someone breathing beside me in the darkness. Cautiously I looked around, my eyes trying to penetrate the darkness; but the fire was almost out and the shadows were too deep for me to be able to distinguish anything.

I edged my way toward the door, expecting at any minute to be attacked. The sound of breathing was still there, pounding in my ears. My hand touched the doorknob, and with a tiny scream, I pulled at it with all my strength.

It wouldn't move!

I sank back down onto the floor, knowing full well I was trapped. The door must be locked from the outside.

After a few minutes spent just sitting in the dark, trying desperately to pull myself together and think of something constructive, I remembered that I had candles in the bottom drawer of the chest. They were ones I'd brought from Aunt Grace's house— special candles that were meant for a celebration; but I needed them now.

Slowly I made my way over to the wall, and with one hand pulled at the drawer, trying to see if anyone was moving toward me. I stopped for a moment; the breathing was still close, and a sob rose to my throat.

"Who are you!" I said. "What are you sitting there in the dark for?"

With a shudder of fear, I thought of Wenna's calm assertion that my mother was coming back to visit me, and chills of horror crept over me. Then I fumbled among my clothes and at last came into contact with one of the candles.

I drew it out of the drawer as noiselessly as possible and crept toward the low fire. If only I could breathe enough life into the embers to get the candle alight!

I thought for a moment I was going to fail, but then the flame shot up and steadied into a good light. I stood up quickly, with my back to the wall, and strained my eyes to accustom them to the flickering light. I couldn't see anyone!

I was calmer now and walked carefully around the room. There was no one, except that there in the middle of my bed was a treasure trove of jewels, pearls, rubies, diamonds, all in a heap like glass beads.

Reaching out, I touched them to make sure they were real. A piece of paper crackled under my fingers, and as I held it nearer to the candle, I saw that it had writing on it. But as it was in Welsh, I had no hope of understanding it. However, I understood the signature all right. It was the Welsh word for "Mother."

I'm not quite clear what I did after that. I think I must have sat there on the bed until morning, just staring at the note and the heap of precious stones and wondering if I was still in my right mind.

At any rate, when there was a loud knocking on the door, I had the presence of mind to pull a cover over the gleaming baubles; and when Greyson came in, smiling and looking refreshed, I tried my best to act normally.

"You might have told me that the tide comes in and fills up those passages," he said. "I only got wet feet, but had there been a high tide, it could have been very nasty for me." He sat down beside me and sniffed the air. "What an odd smell in here. It's almost like incense." He opened a window, then came back and sat beside me. "What's wrong? Didn't you sleep well?"

I pulled back the cover and watched his eyes widen in surprise.

"Apparently my mother paid me another visit last night."

I handed him the note, and suddenly the color left his face. He quickly tucked it into his pocket, and I saw no point in stopping him. I couldn't read it anyway.

"What happened?" he asked calmly, idly picking up a strand of flawless pearls.

I shook my head. "It sounds absurd, but something was wrong with the candles. My eyes were hurting, and then suddenly everything went black." I looked up at him. "When I recovered consciousness, I could hear someone breathing. I'm certain I wasn't alone in here, but there was no light, and by the time I managed to find more candles, whoever it was had gone and these gems were here. I know how silly it must sound, but it's the truth."

Greyson shook his head. "I didn't say it wasn't. I noticed an odd smell when I came in. Perhaps the candles were not the usual ones." He looked around. "Strange, there are no bits left in any of the holders. I presume these two here are the ones you used?"

I nodded excitedly. "Then there was someone in here. Ghosts don't take candles with them, do they?"

Greyson laughed and pinched my cheek. "You are a funny little thing." He bent down and kissed me suddenly. "Don't look so glum. I mean to find out what's going on here, and for a start, I'm moving you out of this room as soon as possible."

I smiled with relief. "That's a good idea," I said, and felt more cheerful.

He put his hand to his lips. "Don't mention it to anyone else. It will be our secret."

He ruffled my hair. "After breakfast, I think you'd better rest for a while. You look quite worn out."

I looked at the jewelry with distaste. "What am I going to do with these?" I said.

"The best thing is to put them in your cupboard with the rest of your things." He kissed my cheek. "Cheer up; Father should be here today. I know you'll be glad to see him and that friend of yours, Edmund. He'll be company for you, won't he?"

"Yes, he will; and it'll be good to see Uncle Tom again."

CHAPTER TEN

It was like a summer's day. The grass had a fresh, rain-washed appearance, and the sky glowed blue through the few puffball clouds that drifted slowly overhead.

I went down into the garden and walked along the small, neat paths. Birds were singing in the dovecote, making the lawns come alive with their enthusiasm, and I felt good just being alive.

Suddenly the chapel bell started to ring, and for a moment I wondered if it was Sunday. Then I saw that the tide was high, reaching almost over the top of the island. Fascinated, I went down to the edge of the garden and watched the water, blue now in the sunshine, swirling around the tree trunks. The stretch of water looked wide and imposing—almost frightening—as it greedily licked the edge of the lawns.

"Amazing, isn't it?" I spun round, startled; I had heard no one approach.

"Edmund, it's you!" From sheer relief, I flung myself into his arms. He looked so handsome, with his bright hair, like gold, and his blue eyes looking down at me.

"How is Uncle Tom?" I leaned away from him, but his arms held me firmly.

"He's better than expected. We broke our journey so that he could rest."

"I see. We were worried by the delay." I smiled and made a more determined effort to escape from Edmund's arms. "I must go to him at once, to see for myself that he is better. Are you coming, Edmund?"

He smiled impishly. "Your uncle is resting. He won't wish to be disturbed just now. But I do."

He bent forward and kissed me lightly, and, laughing, I tried to pull away once more.

"Don't be silly, Edmund. Everyone can see us here," I said in embarrassment.

"So what? That doesn't bother me one little bit. I still hope to make you my wife one of these days."

Some movement drew my eyes past him toward the top of the garden, and I could see Greyson standing quite still, watching. The color came to my face, and I pushed Edmund hard.

"I haven't said yes yet, so please let me go!"

I felt angry, as if I'd been caught doing something wrong, and Edmund looked at me in surprise. Then he turned and saw Greyson, and an understanding smile broke out around his lips. He tucked my arm deliberately under his and led me back up the garden.

"Hello, old chap," he said to Greyson. "Did you want us for anything?"

The two men stared at each other for a moment, and then Greyson turned to me.

"Father is asking to see you, Charlotte, if you can spare a minute."

I bit my lip to stop myself from making an angry retort and, pulling away from Edmund, made my way into the house. To my surprise, Uncle Tom looked much better than I'd expected, and I ran into him and put my arms around him.

"There, there, it's lovely to see you again, my dear." He patted my hair and brushed some loose strands away from my face. "You look more beautiful than ever; I can't tell you how much I've missed you."

I tucked the rug more firmly around his knees. Obviously, in spite of the warmth of the weather, he still felt the chill.

"I'm glad to see you looking better, Uncle. I'll have to look after you very carefully indeed, now that you are here."

He pinched my cheek playfully and winked at me.

"And I shall have to look after you, from what

I've heard," he said quietly. "You must come to my room later and tell me all about it."

I smiled. "I can wait until you are feeling stronger, Uncle."

"Not a bit of it!" he said, and the determination in his voice could not be ignored. "You do as I say, Charlotte. I mean to find out what exactly is happening in my own home."

He put his finger over his lips as Greyson and Edmund came into the room, and I squeezed his hand to show that I understood.

"Would you like a glass of wine, Father?" Greyson held up the bottle, and his father nodded.

"Yes, that would be very nice. Charlotte, how about going into the kitchen and seeing if there is any sweet cake to go with it?"

"Of course, Uncle Tom." I smiled at him. "I won't be a minute."

I made my way quickly to the kitchen, and as I pushed open the door, I could see that there was something going on down at the far end that was engaging everyone's attention. It didn't take me long to discover what it was. Water was seeping in from under the thick flagstones, and most of the younger maids could only try to mop the worst up; their attempts seemed pretty futile.

"What is it?" I asked, and Wenna turned and told me.

"The estuary is almost in flood and is filling the underground passages. It happens occasionally." It seemed as if she suddenly realized it was I. "Oh, Charlotte, is there anything you want?"

She bustled over to the ovens and took out a tray of beautifully baked bread, knocking the crusts with her knuckles to see if the insides were baked enough.

"Uncle Tom would like some sweet cakes, if you have any. Can I get it?"

She smiled. "No, don't worry. I'll get it for you in just a moment."

Deftly she slid the loaves onto a table and covered them with a clean cloth.

"Now what was it? Oh, yes, cake." With a smile, she handed me a silver tray with a variety of sweet things already on it. "I've chosen most of his favorites. Now watch you don't slip on the wet floor."

Puzzled, I left the kitchen and made my way back to the drawing room. How on earth had Wenna known that Uncle Tom would come this morning?"

"Here we are." I handed the tray to Greyson, and he took it to his father.

"Delicious. Cooked just as I liked them. Fill up my glass again, Charlotte, there's a dear."

Greyson and I exchanged glances; mine meant that I thought he'd lied to me about the state of his father's health, and his showed only surprise.

Later, my uncle struggled to his feet, and both

Greyson and Edmund offered their assistance.

"No, Charlotte must come with me."

Uncle Tom smiled, and I took his arm, placing it around my shoulder so that he could lean on me. Slowly and carefully we made our way up the stairs, and I was aware that the two men were watching our progress from the hall.

"Wouldn't they both like to be flies on the wall when we have our little talk?" he said, and I couldn't help smiling.

When he was settled in bed, he bade me come and sit beside him, tapping the spread with his hand.

"Sit here, Charlotte; then I won't have to strain my ears to listen to you," he said.

"All right, Uncle. But honestly, there's not much I can tell you."

I twisted my hands in my lap, wondering what to say. He reached over and smoothed my cheek gently.

"Just tell me everything, however unimportant you may think it is, and I'll know something of what we're up against."

Sadly I looked into his cherubic face. I could never tell him that I was being poisoned and that his son was one of the suspects.

"It's difficult, really. I don't know what's rele-

"Tell me everything," he insisted again.

vant and what is just accident."

"The first thing was Jess's murder." My voice

shook in spite of myself. "That may have been a coincidence, I don't know. She was wearing my cloak at the time."

Uncle nodded. "Go on, dear; tell me the rest."

"There were a number of silly things. I saw lights on the island, and a cross; at least I thought I did."

Uncle Tom's eyebrows rose, but he nodded for me to continue, and he patted my hand once more as if in reassurance.

"Then there was the time I went down under the chapel and someone closed the trap door, so that I was unable to get out again."

"What did you do?" My uncle stared at me, his eyes bright with anger at my predicament.

"I just wandered around, and luckily, I came out near the sea." Not even to my uncle could I say that a hand had taken mine in the darkness and led me out.

"Edmund told me about the balcony breaking suddenly, too suddenly for comfort." Uncle Tom looked at me shrewdly. "That must have been very frightening for you, my dear."

I looked down at my hands, thinking of Fluffy down on the terrace, his tiny body so still and white against the darkness.

"It wasn't one of the better moments of my life," I admitted ruefully. "I had the feeling that it was I who should have been killed—not the kitten!"

"Anything else?" Uncle Tom asked, staring at me intently.

I hesitated, wondering if I should say any more. "I've had presents given me in very mysterious circumstances. Very expensive gifts they were."

"Come on then, Charlotte!" he said, smiling. "Don't keep me in suspense. What have you had?"

"Emeralds, pearls, rubies—that sort of thing. And they've all appeared in my room under mysterious circumstances."

He looked excited. "People have spoken of the riches that were once buried here at the Plas," he said. "It was before your time, when I was a boy and the French were about to invade Wales. It appears that everyone from the surrounding mansions placed their valuables here for safekeeping."

"Well, if that was the case, why weren't the things given back later?"

Uncle Tom shook his head. "Your grandfather died just after the invasion, and no one knew where the things were hidden. Your father and I were just boys. We were more interested in the war that never happened than in other people's fortunes."

"When you grew up, didn't you look?" I asked. "I'm sure I would have searched high and low."

"Oh, we looked. Of course we did. Your father was the legal owner then, and he had many searches organized. It kept the local people quiet, too. They could see for themselves we had no knowledge of the hiding place."

"So why are the valuables turning up now?" I asked suddenly. "It must mean that someone knows where to look."

He nodded. "I agree with you, Charlotte. And if they can be found, they must be given back to their rightful owners, or their heirs, don't you agree?"

"Yes, of course, Uncle. But how are we going to find out who they are?"

He tapped his eyelids. "By keeping these open, Charlotte. That's the only way."

"Uncle Tom," I said suddenly, "why on earth would anyone want me dead?"

His bushy eyebrows drew together in a frown. "I can't tell you that, my dear child. I can't even believe it's true. But don't worry; you'll be safe with me here."

He leaned back against the pillows then, and I rose, seeing that he was tired.

"I'm sorry, Uncle; I shouldn't have stayed so long."

I bent forward and kissed his forehead, and he smiled affectionately at me.

"That's all right, Charlotte; you just keep me informed of everything that happens. And I'd like to see your gifts when you've got a minute to show them to me."

Quietly I let myself out of the room and met Wenna, who was just bringing tea.

"Uncle is sleepy. I'd leave it until later if I were you," I said with a smile.

She didn't even bother to answer. She brushed past me, walked into my uncle's room without even knocking and closed the door in my surprised face.

"Conference over?" Edmund was at the foot of the stairs, smiling up at me.

"What do you know about it?" I said with a sudden unexplained hostility.

"Your uncle confides in me a great deal. I meant no harm."

He looked so crestfallen that I had to smile. I took his arm, and together we walked back to the drawing room, where Greyson was sitting in gloomy silence. He looked up at us, his dark eyes unfathomable.

I disengaged my arm from Edmund's and sat down, feeling drained of energy.

"May I have a glass of wine, please, Greyson? I asked meekly.

He got to his feet in one movement, looking lithe and tall beside Edmund's stocky breadth. His hair was crisp and dark, springing away from his face, and his eyes were half closed as he stared down at the ruby wine.

I took the glass with trembling fingers and avoided looking directly at Greyson as he sat beside me.

"What did Father have to say? You were with him quite a long time."

He leaned toward me, offering a piece of cake, but I shook my head.

"Oh, nothing very important, really." I hated myself for telling him lies, but I could hardly tell him the truth. "He's resting now, although Wenna insisted on taking him tea."

Greyson nodded. "Yes, that's her daily ritual when he's here. She looks after him like a baby."

I couldn't help wondering if something was being put into Uncle Tom's tea. It would explain why he had been ill when he had first arrived at Winston.

"You are far away," Greyson remarked. "What were you thinking about?"

"Uncle Tom's health. He seems much better, don't you think?"

Edmund was determined to break into the conversation. He pulled his chair nearer to mine and leaned forward.

"Oh, yes, he's been improving steadily these last few weeks, didn't you know?"

I looked at him and then at Greyson, who seemed suddenly tense, though he hadn't moved at all.

"On the contrary," I said stiffly, "I thought he was worse."

Greyson leaned forward and looked intently at Edmund. "But you sent William down with a message to tell me Father was worse," he said firmly.

Edmund shook his head in bewilderment. "No, I did not!" He turned to me. "Did you see William, Charlotte?"

I was forced to shake my head. "I didn't see him, but Greyson told me he was here."

"Well, let's send for him. I'm sure he can clear this up in no time." Edmund beamed, and I sighed with relief.

"Of course. Why don't you ring the bell, Greyson? There must be some misunderstanding."

Greyson leaned back, an odd smile on his face. "I don't think there has been any misunderstanding," he said thoughtfully. "I think I've been made a fool of!"

"Greyson, what do you mean?" I asked indignantly. "William wouldn't attempt to make a fool of you."

He shook his head. "Maybe not, but he's disappeared. He didn't say a word—just vanished."

I put my hand to my lips. "Oh, Greyson, I do hope he's all right."

Edmund coughed and got to his feet. "Ah, well, no doubt there is some explanation; but I can't think of one at the moment."

"Except that I am a liar, is that what you are getting at?" Greyson glared at Edmund and moved closer to him.

"I didn't say anything." Edmund looked defiantly at me, and I stepped in quickly.

"There can be no good purpose served by quarreling. Will both of you sit down again?"

I stood with my hands on my hips and out-stared the two of them, though my legs were trembling. When they were seated, I poured drinks for the three of us and sat down between them.

"I, for one, believe that William was here," I said. "And if he has disappeared without a word, something is wrong, very wrong." I looked at Greyson. "William was very loyal to me. I've known him for a long time. He wouldn't leave without seeing me unless he was forced to."

Greyson looked back at me, his eyes unreadable. "I think it's time I went to bed," he said flatly, rose and went outside. He stopped at the door and called me. "Could you spare me a minute, Charlotte?" he said imperiously.

Edmund grimaced, and I felt the color rise to my cheeks as I went to the door.

"Here is the key to your new room," Greyson said quietly. "Leave most of your belongings where they are for now, so no one will guess you are moving."

"Where is my room?" I asked curiously, and suddenly he smiled.

"I hope you won't mind, but you've got one of the maids' rooms. Will that be all right?"

I nodded. "But Wenna brings me tea every morning. What shall I do about that?"

"I'll make sure she sees to Uncle and friend Edmund first. That will give you time to get back to your own room and rumple the bed."

I smiled. "All right, Greyson, and thank you. See you in the morning."

Edmund was sulking when I returned to him. He stared down at the floor for a long time until, with a sigh, I challenged him.

"What's wrong now, Edmund?" I sat near him, and he looked up at me reproachfully.

"You are far too friendly with Greyson for my liking. I don't trust that fellow."

"He is my cousin, Edmund," I said quietly. "Come on; cheer up. Perhaps we will be able to go out for a walk together tomorrow, if the weather stays fine."

Edmund was not to be side-tracked. "He was not speaking one word of truth. You realize that, don't you?"

"Why do you say that?" I asked impatiently. "Will must have been here."

"No, he's at Winston. He's never left there, not even for one day."

"Are you sure about that, Edmund?" I could feel the color leaving my cheeks. I wanted with all my heart to believe in Greyson.

"Charlotte, is it a thing I could make a mistake

about? Anyway, you can ask him yourself when we get back."

"Get back? Do you mean Uncle is going back to Winston?" I said. "I thought he wanted to be here."

"You are deliberately being stupid, Charlotte. When you and I go back as man and wife, that's what I meant."

"Now wait a minute, Edmund. I haven't said I'd marry you, have I?"

"You are splitting hairs, Charlotte. It's always been understood we'd marry one day."

I sighed. "I'm rather tired, Edmund. I think I'd better get some sleep."

To my dismay, he came upstairs with me and stood outside my room. Reluctantly, I opened the door and let myself in, standing just inside the door, listening to his footsteps going away.

The fire was lit and candles burned in their holders; naturally, everyone assumed I was still using the room. The curtains over the balcony door billowed a little, and then I felt the hairs rise on the back of my neck, and I went absolutely cold. There was a woman standing in the gloom, wearing a black dress and with waist-length dark hair.

I couldn't move. I could barely breathe. I stood rooted·to the spot with fear. She stood staring at me, and then she began to raise her arms, and I saw her lips frame my name, though no sound came out.

Slowly, as if in a nightmare, she began to move toward me. She stood poised for a moment under the candlelight, and to my horror, I saw there was seaweed clinging to her hair.

From somewhere I found the strength to move. I pulled at the door and ran onto the landing, screaming Greyson's name, and then there were hands holding me as I sank into blessed darkness. . . .

CHAPTER ELEVEN

A cup was pressed to my lips, and I gasped as hot tea spilled onto my face. I took the cup with hands that shook uncontrollably and looked at the sea of faces around me.

Greyson held me in his arms, and Uncle Tom, his face white, was kneeling on the floor beside me. Edmund was returning the cup to the tray Wenna was holding in her hands.

I stared hard at Wenna. The woman looked like her, so very much like her! But Wenna was in her nightgown, with her hair tidily hidden under a cap. Could it have been my mother I had seen?

"Feeling better?" Greyson asked, holding me up in a sitting position.

I nodded. "Yes, thank you. If you'll help me up, I'll be all right. I'm sorry I've disturbed you all. Won't you go back to bed?"

Greyson took charge. "Wenna, perhaps you and Edmund will take Father to his room, and I'll see to Charlotte."

At the tone of command in his voice, everyone began to move away.

"What was it?" he asked. "Something frightened you, didn't it?"

"Greyson, are you sure my mother is dead?" I asked, and even to myself, my question sounded silly.

"Why, yes, she was drowned. I can even remember her a little. Why do you ask?"

I shook my head. "I thought I saw her tonight. She was standing near the balcony of my room, and she held her hands out to me. It was horrible!"

Greyson frowned. "But it's impossible. No one can get in that way. The balcony hasn't been repaired."

"I know, I know, that's why it's all so mad!" I leaned against him, feeling desperately ill. "Greyson, I think I'm going out of my mind," I said, and tears slid down my cheeks.

"Wait here," he said. "I'm going to have a look."

I stood against the wall, watching in fear as he opened the door to my room. I saw him go across to the curtain and move it aside, and then he disappeared from view as he searched around the bed. He returned in a few moments with a necklace dangling from his hands.

"Another one," he said darkly. "And there's no sign of anyone having broken in."

"Could it be a ghost?" I asked in a small voice. "I saw something—I know I did."

He took my arm. "Come along; you've had enough

to put up with for one night. You'll be safe upstairs."

He took me into the attic room, and it was a relief to be in a small room where there were no dark corners and large recesses; just long beams bending like crooked arms across the tiny slanting ceiling. He turned his back until I was in bed and then sat beside me.

"Look, Charlotte," he said, "try to put everything out of your mind. Promise?"

I grinned wryly. "I promise to try; but it won't be easy, will it?"

He pulled the covers up to my chin. "Would you like me to stay with you, just for tonight? I can sit in the rocking chair and make sure no one comes in."

I smiled. "And what will Edmund and your father make of that? No, thank you, Greyson. You'd better go to your own room. I think I'll be all right here."

"Good night, then." He bent forward and kissed me gently. "I'll see you in the morning. If you should need me tonight, just knock on the floor. My room is directly under yours."

I lay for a long time staring at the cracks in the ceiling above me and praying for daylight to come.

Uncle Tom was still resting in his room the next morning, and I offered to take some tea up to him.

"Hello, my dear; come and sit down." He smiled

and patted the bed. "I hope you are feeling better today."

"Yes, I'm fine, thank you, Uncle. Do you want some tea?"

I handed him the cup and sat down at his side, happy to see that he looked much better. There was color in his face again, and I realized that last night I must have frightened him badly."

I'd wanted to question him about William, but it didn't seem to be very kind to worry him under the circumstances.

"What are you thinking?" he said, patting my hand gently. He leaned back on the pillows and smiled, and for the first time since I'd known him it occurred to me that he wasn't really an old man, in spite of his silver hair and bushy brows.

"I'm just thinking how handsome you look." I smiled warmly and tweaked his nose. "You should be out enjoying the company of some eligible ladies. They must be ten a penny in these parts."

"Maybe you are right, Charlotte, but it's Greyson they are all after. He could have been married three times over by now."

My heart dipped in the oddest way, and for some reason I couldn't look at my uncle.

"Of course I would like to see him married to you. I'm very fond of you, my dear. But I think that Edmund has first refusal, isn't that correct?"

I sighed. "Poor Edmund! He keeps asking me to marry him, but I don't think it would work."

"Ah! Well, you have my sympathy; but it's not every young lady who has two fine young men begging for her hand. And don't forget, Charlotte, there is the danger of falling between two stools."

"I'm just not ready for marriage yet. I can't imagine settling down and having children. It all seems far away in the future."

I moved the tray and straightened the cover of Uncle's bed.

"You'd better rest now, and then perhaps we'll have the pleasure of your company this evening at supper."

"I expect so, Charlotte. And think over what I've said. Don't turn down any offer out of hand. You may regret it later."

There seemed to be some underlying meaning in my uncle's words that I couldn't fathom. I stopped for a moment on the landing and tried to work out what he could have meant. It sounded as if he were advising me to marry Edmund, and yet he'd told me himself he'd like me to accept Greyson. I grimaced wryly. I couldn't even be sure that Greyson would have me.

As I passed the door of my room, something made me stop. Carefully I pushed the handle, and the door swung open. The bed was made, and the fire grate had been carefully cleaned out, so that a fire could be lit at night. It all seemed so harmless, with the sun streaming in through the window, that I couldn't believe anything at all had happened last night.

In my cupboard was the new necklace, along with all the other valuables, just placed carelessly in a box as if they were of no importance. Idly I lifted them up, and they shot bright fires across my skin. They were beautiful, priceless stones, and yet I wished I'd never seen them.

I jumped, startled, as I heard soft footsteps behind me. Then Wenna appeared.

"Oh, Charlotte, the maid tells me you didn't sleep in here last night. I'm not surprised, seeing you were so upset, though I've told you before that your mother wouldn't harm you. She just wants you to be happy."

She spoke quite normally, as if my mother were alive, and uneasily I moved away from her.

"What was my mother like? To look at, I mean? Was she like me, for instance?"

Wenna shook her head. "No, not like you at all, except perhaps about the eyes. But she was very lovable; such charming ways. I couldn't believe it when she drowned."

"Wenna, did you see her? I mean after she was found out there?" I gestured toward the island, not quite sure how to say it without upsetting Wenna.

She shook her head bitterly. "Oh, no, I couldn't

look at her, Miss Charlotte; it was too much for me."

Even now, at the thought, tears welled in her eyes, and I felt ashamed, like someone uncovering an old wound.

"I'm sorry, Wenna; I didn't mean to upset you. I just wondered about it, that's all."

She didn't speak again for a few minutes. She walked across to the window and stood looking out at the sea.

"It's natural to ask about your mother, quite natural. And she was somebody special all right, even though they say she was a bad lot, because she wasn't married to your father." She turned to look at me, her eyes rather dazed. "For a while I believed they were married. I even remember the cermony in the chapel, and the bell ringing out joyfully to tell all the world." She stopped speaking and put her hand over her eyes. "But it seems it was all inside my head. I was ill for a long time after she died."

"Who told you there was no marriage, Wenna? Can you remember?"

Her eyes cleared as she heard my voice, and she looked at me suspiciously.

"Why are you questioning me like this, miss! I haven't done anything wrong."

"Wenna," I said slowly, "I'm not saying you have done anything wrong. I was only asking about my mother." I tried to smile. "And what's this nonsense about you calling me 'miss'? You've never done it befor."

She looked down at her fingers, her brows drawn together in an uncharacteristic frown.

"Your uncle's orders. He doesn't like me to be familiar. He told me off about it."

I raised my eyebrows in surprise. "But I don't mind at all. After all, you are one of the family, aren't you?"

She smiled thinly. "Well, he doesn't like it, and he's the master here, even though Greyson does all the managing, and on precious little money at that."

"Do you mean that Uncle Tom is short of money?" I couldn't believe it. Plas Melyn was run on much more luxurious lines than Winston.

"That's about it, miss. Trouble is, he doesn't know it." She moved toward the door. "Greyson says he must never know. It would kill him."

"Then who pays for everything?" I asked, puzzled by the whole thing.

"Greyson does! By right he owns the Plas and has for these many years. Good thing he had money left him by his mother's side of the family."

"It will all be his one day," I said comfortingly. "I'm sure it's money well spent in the long run."

"I dare say you are right." She opened the door, determined to answer no more questions, and reluctantly I had to let her go."

"Well," I said softly, "who'd have thought Greyson would be so generous?"

By evening Uncle Tom seemed to be in excellent spirits. He sat at the head of the table and kept everyone amused with his tall stories about smugglers coming into the estuary with gold and kegs of wine; anything, in fact, that would bring a fair price from the people living near the coast.

"Yes, they used to flash lights from the island out there, and then the rowboats would come in like a fleet of dark beetles, and there would be gentlemen and ladies wading out into the water in their hurry to have the best pickings."

I drank more wine and smiled indulgently. Uncle was quite obviously enjoying himself. His cheeks were pink, so that he looked more than ever like a cherub. And his hair was brushed until it shone like silk.

"Where's Wenna tonight?" Edmund said conversationally, when Uncle at last lapsed into silence.

It was Greyson who answered. "I don't think she's feeling very well," he said almost protectively.

"Nonsense!" Uncle beamed at me jovially. "Go and bring her in, Charlotte. She must eat with us tonight. I insist."

I rose, but Greyson was at the door before me.

"I'll see how she is. Don't worry. You enjoy your supper."

Something niggled in the back of my mind, but I couldn't think what it was that made me so uneasy. I returned to my seat and accepted the wine that Uncle offered me.

"Well, Charlotte, have you made up your mind about marriage yet?" Uncle smiled mischievously at me and then at Edmund, and suddenly I was angry.

"No, I have not. And I don't think it's anyone else's business, quite honestly!"

I could have bitten out my tongue as soon as the words were out, because Uncle looked so crestfallen. Silently he poured himself another drink.

"I'm sorry, Uncle," I said quickly. "I must be tired, that's all."

"Yes, of course, my dear. And quite right, too. I'm an intefering old man." He paused. "It's just that I want to see you settled—just in case anything happens to me."

I hurried to his side and put my arms around him. "Oh, Uncle, don't talk like that. Nothing is going to happen to you." I felt tears fill my eyes as I kissed his round cheek. "And you needn't worry about me. I promise I'll make up my mind quite soon."

Greyson returned and closed the door quietly behind him. If he was surprised to see me clinging to his father, my eyes damp, he didn't say anything.

Feeling a little foolish, I sat down again, and Uncle Tom managed a smile. "All right now, Charlotte, don't forget your promise. I'll hold you to it."

Greyson's eyes were on my face, and carefully I looked down at my plate.

"Isn't Wenna going to join us after all?" I said, anxious to change the subject.

"She really isn't well," Greyson said, and I could tell he was concerned. "I think she's caught some sort of chill. Her temperature is certainly up."

"Oh, can I take her something, do you think?" I asked eagerly, but he shook his head.

"No, it's all been taken care of. She needs to be kept warm and to have plenty of rest. She's been working too hard."

"Poor Wenna. I'll drop in to see her before I go to bed," Uncle Tom said softly. "I take her so much for granted. She's been part of the Plas for so long. I couldn't imagine it without her."

"I'd leave it until the morning if I were you, Father." Greyson spoke quietly, but there was almost a command in his voice.

"Perhaps you are right. You usually are."

He smiled at his son, and I wondered why there was no answering smile from Greyson. Was it possible that he resented continually pouring money into his father's property?

"I think I'll go up to bed, if everyone will excuse

me." I smiled at Uncle and moved away, and Edmund jumped up to open the door for me.

"Good night, Charlotte, my dear," he said, and bent over my hand in such a proprietary way that I felt angry with him. Abruptly I said good night and marched out into the hall.

I didn't go straight upstairs, however. I flung on my cloak and went outside into the cool night air. The stars were brilliant in the clear sky, and the gentle slap-slap of the water had a soothing quality about it.

Picking my way carefully, I went down the steps and sat for a moment in the dimness of the dovecote; but I felt shut in, and once more I walked along the damp grass, drawn in some strange way toward the sea.

"Restless, too, I see." I jumped as Greyson came up behind me suddenly and put his arms around my shoulders. "Do you think it is safe for you to be alone like this?" he asked teasingly.

"I don't really think my mother means me any harm," I said, trying to be flippant.

He drew me close to him and tipped back my head so that I was forced to look at him.

"Charlotte, are you really seeing these things, or is it just an excuse to cover up something you've found?"

I was already tired and harassed, and his questions were just too much. Fingers of anger crept up inside me, and I pulled away from him so suddenly that he had no alternative but to let me go.

"Sometimes I think I hate you!" I said fiercely, and started to run as fast as I could down the lawn toward the sea.

"Charlotte, come back. Don't be a fool!"

Greyson's voice was urgent, but I took no notice. I couldn't think of anything but the bitterness inside me. I'd been believing in him, even starting to trust him, and all the time he still had had his doubts about my integrity.

I could hear him running behind him.

"Charlotte, come here!" he shouted, but his anger only spurred me on.

I could see that he was gaining on me, and there didn't seem anywhere to go. Suddenly, for no apparent reason, I was more frightened than I'd ever been. From the sea came a strange scent, like something rotting. I screamed, and then my foot caught in a root, and I pitched forward just as a shot rang out behind me.

There was a burning agony in my shoulder, and I was thrust forward as if by a mighty hand; and the waves reached up like black arms and drew me down into their cool darkness.

CHAPTER TWELVE

Sunlight was streaming into the room, teasing my eyelids and making me sneeze. "Oh!" I exclaimed, as the pain in my shoulder brought me to full consciousness.

Uncle Tom was smiling down at me, and his hand was warm over mine.

"My dear child, thank God you are all right."

He leaned over and kissed my cheek, and I realized I was stretched flat on the bed with no pillows under my head.

"What's wrong with me?" I asked, bewildered. As I tried to sit up, Uncle Tom gently pushed me back, forcing me to lie down.

"Don't exert yourself, Charlotte. You have been very ill. Don't you remember anything?"

It all came back to me then in a picture as clear as if I'd just awakened from a nightmare: the dark sea, Greyson behind me, and the shot that sent me pitching forward into darkness. I stared at my uncle, a question in my eyes. He looked away in distress and forced himself to speak.

"There has been no sign of Greyson since the night

he shot you." He brushed a shaking hand over his eyes. "I can't believe it of my own son."

"But Greyson wouldn't do a thing like that!" I exclaimed. "What would be his motive?"

"I really don't know, Charlotte. I can't understand it. I thought he wanted to marry you."

"It must have been someone else, Uncle. It just doesn't make any sense."

He shook his head gravely. "I'm afraid there is no doubt about it. Edmund saw it all. That's how we got to you so quickly; otherwise you would have drowned."

Tears spilled over my cheeks. There was an intolerable ache inside me. I loved Greyson, and I couldn't believe he would harm me.

"But why? Just answer me that. Why would he want me dead?"

Uncle Tom moved away and looked through the window. "In the beginning, he tried to prove that you were an impostor. Do you know why he did that?"

Uncle Tom didn't look at me, and it seemed as if he spoke against his will.

"He thought there was some property that belonged to me," I said, "and he wanted to make sure I was really his cousin before he allowed me to have it."

"Do you know what that property was?" Uncle Tom turned to look at me, his face drawn. "It was

Plas Melyn itself and all inside the grounds. That meant the treasure, if it exists; and there has been some proof of that since you came here."

It took me a moment to digest this information, but I still couldn't see why Greyson should try to kill me.

"But he had Winston, which was all I ever wanted; and the Plas is yours, Uncle. Everyone knows that."

He shook his head. "It's mine to live in until my death, but the deeds are in your name, child. It was your father's wish."

I was beginning to see now. "And if I died, Greyson would naturally benefit?"

He nodded. "Yes; he would have been next in line after you. He was the only other heir. There were only the two of you."

My voice shook. "Where can he be now?" I looked across the blue expanse of sky outside the window, and it was as if life had lost all its meaning.

"I suppose he's gone back to Winston. There's nothing anyone can do. We could never prove he tried to murder you."

I shuddered. "I wouldn't want to do that, Uncle. I'd much rather let him go. I still can't believe he meant to hurt me."

He shook his head. "Greed is a very strong emotion, Charlotte. I'm only sorry you've had to learn that the hard way."

There was a knock on the door, and Edmund looked in. He smiled in delight as he saw I was conscious.

"Charlotte, are you feeling better now?" He came and knelt at the bedside and kissed my cheek, holding my hand tightly in his. "I'm sorry everything has turned out like this, Charlie, but once you are strong again, we'll be married, and I'll be able to look after you always."

I tried to smile. "Dear Edmund, you are always there when I need you." My eyes were growing heavy so that I could barely keep them open. "I'm so tired," I murmured. And then there was nothing but the sound of soft soothing waves overwhelming me in darkness.

It was warm on the terrace, and the fact that my arm was in a sling didn't prevent me from arranging the charming posy of flowers that Edmund had brought me from Graig Melyn.

"I must take you for a drive one of these days," he said, smiling down at me. "Your shoulder is almost completely healed now. Wenna swears it's the effect of the salt water that's made you heal so quickly. In a few weeks you will be fit enough to ride in the coach."

I nodded absently. I had not the slightest wish to go into town. All I wanted to do was sit in the peaceful gardens and avoid thinking about anything.

"Charlotte, are you listening? You seem to be so far away these days. There's no reaching you."

"Yes, I'm listening," I said, without raising my eyes from the bright flowers.

He sighed and took a seat near me. "Look at me, Charlotte," he said firmly. "You can leave those for a minute or two. I want to talk to you."

I felt a twinge of irritation at his tone, but I was too weary to argue with him. Obediently I left the flowers and sat back in my chair attentively.

"That's better," he said more gently. "Now you know how much I love you. I don't have to keep telling you. I've been asking you to marry me for a long time now—far too long—and I'm tired of being put off."

He took my hand in his and looked down at me, his blue eyes bright and full of warmth.

"Remember, I saved your life, Charlotte. Doesn't that prove how much I love you?"

"Yes, Edmund, of course it does." I tried my best to sound grateful, but I really was too weary to care one way or the other.

"Why not marry me, then? Let me take care of you always?"

I stared at him listlessly for a moment, and somehow it seemed easier to give in than to listen to his arguments.

"All right, Edmund, if it will make you happy. I will marry you, if Uncle Tom will give his permission, of course."

Edmund beamed and kissed me on the cheek. "He'll be only too delighted to see you settled. Don't worry about that, Charlotte. I'll go and tell him. After all, he should be the first to know."

When he'd gone, I got up and walked down to the dovecote and sat inside, cocooned from the world, hidden from view, isolated. All I wanted was to be left in peace. Why would no one leave me to myself?

I was still there some time later when Wenna came to call me for tea. She stood looking down at me, her eyes unfathomable.

"Is it true you are going to marry Mr. Edmund?" she said softly.

"What did he say?" With difficulty I concentrated on what she was saying. "Oh, that. Yes, I suppose so."

I sat motionless until she caught my arm and led me up the garden steps and onto the terrace. The shadows were long on the lawn, and the cool air made me shiver.

"Come inside," she said kindly. "I'll serve tea in front of the fire today." She saw me comfortably settled and put more fuel on the flames. "You are doing the wrong thing, Miss Charlotte," she said calmly. "You shouldn't marry him; he's wrong for you. I know it."

I sat staring into the fire; there didn't seem to be anything I could say.

She clucked her tongue in exasperation and went out to the kitchen. Uncle Tom spoke a few words to her as he came in, though I couldn't catch what he said.

"My dear Charlotte—" he came up to me and put his arm around my shoulder—"Edmund has told me the good news. I can't tell you how pleased I am that you will be looked after when I'm gone."

I tried to smile. "But you will stay with us, Uncle," I said slowly, won't you?"

He patted my hand. "You misunderstand me, Charlotte. I meant that I won't always be on this earth to look after you." He sat down. "Well, never mind that. When will the great day be?"

"I don't mind, Uncle. I'll leave everything to you and Edmund. I don't think I've quite gotten over the shock, but I'll be all right soon."

"That's the spirit. I'm sure you and Edmund will be very happy."

"What about Greyson?" I asked, and my voice broke suddenly.

Uncle Tom went white, his eyebrows drew together in a frown, and I knew I shouldn't have spoken.

"Please, Charlotte, if you want to spare me pain, don't mention that name to me again."

"But he is your son and my cousin. We can't just write him off like that! Have you made any inquiries about his whereabouts?"

"Excuse me; I'll go and bring in the tea."

He rose and left the room without another word, and I wondered where my sudden spurt of energy had come from. I got to my feet and looked out at the darkening lawn. The island seemed to be beckoning to me, even though there was no one in sight. The water lapped softly around it, isolating it so well.

Had I really agreed to marry Edmund? It all seemed far away and hazy, and I felt a qualm of fear as I realized how big a step I was taking.

As if conjured up by my thoughts, he came into the room, a roll of silk under his arm.

"How would you like a dress made of this, Charlotte?" His eyes shone as he spread the thick, creamy material before me.

Indifferently I looked down at it. "Yes, it would be very charming."

"Very well; that's what you shall wear at the wedding. It's decided."

Briskly he folded the roll of silk again. Just then, before I could frame a reply, there was a tap on the door, and Wenna brought in the tea.

My throat was dry. I longed to tell Edmund that I'd made a mistake. I couldn't go through with it after all. Nervously I watched him come and sit beside me and hand me a cup. I almost flinched away as he leaned forward and patted my cheek.

"We'll be so happy together. I'll take you away from here. Everything will be fine, you'll see."

He handed me a cup, and I took it, grateful for something to occupy my hands. I wanted to tell him, but with his face shining and full of enthusiasm, I couldn't bring myself to do it.

"Where's Uncle Tom?" I asked quietly. "Perhaps I could tell *him* how I felt, and then he would help me to extricate myself from a difficult position.

"He's resting. Something seems to have upset him. But don't worry; Wenna will look after him. You just stay with me and concentrate on our plans for the future." He smiled. "You've never liked it here, have you, Charlotte? I don't blame you one little bit, after all that's happened."

He settled back in his chair and stretched his feet out, resting them on a stool.

"I don't really know what to say, Edmund. I've always loved Winston, of course, but to go and live near there now, with my cousin in residence—I don't think I could bear it."

He looked at me blankly for a moment, and then seemed to realize what I was talking about.

"Yes, I see it could be difficult. I didn't think, I'm afraid." His speech seemed to be slightly slurred, and suddenly he put his hand over his mouth to smother a yawn. "Oh, excuse me. It's unpardonably rude of me to yawn. I just seem to be suddenly tired."

His eyelids drooped, and soon I could tell by his regular breathing that he was asleep.

Carefully I leaned forward and tasted the dregs of his tea, grimacing at the bitterness that lingered in my mouth. It was drugged, there was no doubt about it! And I became certain in that moment that I had been given large doses of the stuff myself. How otherwise could I explain the apathy that had held me in its grip and made me agree to marry Edmund rather than argue with him?

I thought back to the time when I was slowly being poisoned, when I had been ill. I had lost weight and felt a revulsion against any sort of food. This drug was something else; it sapped the will and left its victim so tired that everything seemed too much trouble.

But why Edmund? And who could be administering the drug? I brushed my hair back from my eyes and went quietly into the kitchen. Perhaps I would be able to find something incriminating there, so that I could confront Wenna with it.

The creak of the doors as I opened them echoed so loudly it seemed as if the whole house must know what I was doing. It would be dangerous to get caught. I had no illusions about that. There was someone at the Plas who was very dangerous, and I could expect no help from Edmund. He would sleep for hours before the effect of the drug wore off.

After about an hour, I still had found nothing at all suspicious. I dipped my hands in flour bags and salt barrels, and everything was as it should be. I suppose it was foolish of me to think that such things would be left out in the open where anyone could use them accidentally.

Edmund was still sleeping. I draped a rug over him and went up to my room. There was nothing I could do for him at the moment. He would wake up when the drug had worn off, and then I could tell him what had happened.

I was still sleeping in the small attic room where Greyson had put me. I suppose it was silly to think I was any safer there than anywhere else, especially now I knew Greyson had wanted me dead. But all the same, I liked the way the roof bent downward, almost as if it were a protection, and the small proportions of the room made for fewer shadows.

I lay for a long time, awake in the candlelight, straining my ears for the faintest sound of Edmund coming up the stairs. Then, so suddenly that it startled me, there was a knock on the door.

"Come in!" I said. But when the door opened, it was not Edmund but my uncle who stood there.

"Charlotte, my dear, you are in bed early this

evening. And Edmund is asleep in a chair down in the drawing room. There must be something to this talk of marriage that makes you young folks sleepy." He smiled and sat beside me. "I'm sorry, child, if I seemed a bit short-tempered with you earlier. It's just that I can't bear even to think of Greyson, do you understand?"

"I was thoughtless to mention him. I'm the one who should be sorry."

I wondered how I could broach the subject of the drugs. Perhaps it would be wrong of me even to try. Uncle Tom wasn't very strong, and he'd had enough shocks lately. Smiling, I took his hand in mine.

"Poor Uncle, I've been nothing but trouble to you ever since you set eyes on me!"

Smiling, he shook his head vigorously. "Nonsense! You must not talk like that. You've brought me fresh hope in my old age."

"I'm glad to hear I've been of some use, though I don't think I can agree with you." I kissed his cheek. "Is there anything I can get you before you go to bed?"

He smiled at me with an impish expression. "I wouldn't mind some sweet cake and a glass of wine, if you are going to get something for yourself."

"Yes, I am going to get something for myself. I've just decided I'm hungry!"

There was no sign of Wenna anywhere in the downstairs rooms. The house was strangely silent, for, although it was dark, it was really quite early, and no one had been given any supper.

I took a candlestick with me and pushed open the kitchen door. Everything was as I'd left it earlier—neat, orderly, and empty of any activity.

I'd been stupid not to think of it before, but I suppose I'd still been in a semi-drugged state. By now there should be pies baked for the weekend and bread, smelling fresh and crusty, in the larder, but the shelves were bare. What on earth could be happening? Surely all the maids and cooks couldn't have been dismissed.

It didn't take me long to get my uncle his drink of wine, but he would have to do without his cake until another day.

I looked in at Edmund and saw he was still sleeping peacefully, his hair flopping over his eyes just like a little boy's. I tucked the rug more firmly around his shoulders and went back up the stairs.

"Uncle Tom." I tapped on his door softly. "I've brought your wine."

He was tucked up in bed like a round-faced cherub, waiting with anticipation for his wine and cake. I gave him the wine and wrapped my robe firmly around myself, trying to pluck up the courage to tell him what I'd learned.

"Uncle Tom, everyone has gone! We seem to be alone in the house. Not even Wenna is here."

He looked at me through startled eyes over the rim of his glass. "Perhaps they are all in bed, Charlotte. An early night, just like us."

I shook my head. "No, Uncle, the larder is empty. There's been no cooking done for the weekend, and you know none of the cooks will bake on Sunday."

He scratched his silver hair, looking as perplexed as I felt.

"What could have happened to them?" His voice trembled, and I felt an almost overwhelming pity for him. He was like a bewildered child, punished for something he hadn't done.

"Perhaps they've walked out for some reason. They may think there's a danger of being shot at. I'm sorry to mention it, Uncle, but it is a possibility."

"What can be done? Can't you go and wake young Edmund?" He swung his thin legs over the edge of the bed. "Yes, why didn't I think of that before? Let's go and get him."

"All right, Uncle, but put something warm on. I don't want you catching a chill on top of all this."

Together we went down the stairs, and uneasily I held the candle high, looking from side to side. There was an unnatural silence in the old house. All the usual creaks and groans seemed to have stopped, as if by magic.

Slowly I led my uncle into the drawing room, and such was the state of my nerves that I was surprised to see Edmund still sitting in the chair where I'd left him, though the rug had slipped to the floor.

"You wake him up, Charlotte. This is no time for sleeping." Uncle Tom stood before the dying fire. "I think I'll just stir this up a bit and add some coal and logs. It's going to be a cold night, and the dratted thing will only have to be relit in the morning if I allow it to go out now."

I smiled indulgently as Uncle fussed ineffectively around the grate.

"Here, let me." I took the tongs from him and built the fire up, brushing the hearth so that it looked neat again. "Wenna would have a fit if she saw the place untidy," I said before I realized that Wenna was no longer there.

"Oh, well, I dare say we'll manage until we can get someone else up here to work."

Uncle Tom went over to Edmund and shook him by the shoulder.

"Come on, young fellow; this is no time to sleep."

There was no answer. Edmund's head lolled awkwardly to one side. With a feeling of dread in my throat, I moved closer and with an effort stopped myself from screaming out. The dose of drugs in Edmund's cup must have been a lethal one, because he was dead.

CHAPTER THIRTEEN

Somehow I helped Uncle Tom upstairs and settled him in a chair. He leaned back, looking pale and tired.

"In the morning we must go into town and get help," I said, rubbing my hands together, trying to bring a little warmth into them.

Uncle Tom started to cough violently. "My medicine please, Charlotte."

He pointed to the rosewood chest, and, alarmed, I hurriedly lifted the top and searched about among the bottles and jars for his medicine.

Suddenly I noticed a small cloth bag tied at the top with green ribbon. Scrawled across it in red ink was one word, "Poison." Deftly I opened it and dabbed some of the powder onto my finger. It tasted bitter, similar to the dregs of Edmund's tea.

I moved a few more bottles and saw a rolled-up piece of paper, and when I unfolded it the word "Bradwr" stared up at me.

"For your information, Charlotte, it means 'traitor.' Your father's name for me! He wasn't as easy to dupe as you've been."

Uncle Tom was standing behind me, a gun pointing at my back. I could scarcely believe my senses.

"Did you kill Edmund?" I whispered.

"Unfortunately. He became too ambitious! He wanted to marry you before I had found the jewels. Legally, they would have been his then. You do see I had no choice, don't you?"

"Do you mean he was working for you?"

Uncle Tom must have heard the disbelief in my voice, because he chuckled. "Of course he was! I'm sorry I had to dispense with his services."

Slowly I turned round. "But why did he turn against me?" I asked bitterly.

"My dear child," my uncle said, "he liked the thought of all that wealth."

"Oh, Uncle, you don't even know if there is any wealth here."

I was playing for time, frantically wondering how I could escape.

"Oh, yes, you have some of it in your room; and now you can lead me to the rest of the valuables."

"I don't know where those things came from. They just appeared in my room."

"Don't try to fox me with your talk about ghosts, Charlotte. I'll admit it was a good story to cover up what you were doing. You even had me fooled for a time. I suppose the map is in your room?"

"Map? What map?" I put my hand to my head in despair. "Uncle, I have no idea what you are talking about."

"The map to the underground passages, of course!" he said, as if explaining a lesson to a difficult child. "Edmund told me how you found your way out of there."

I turned away and pressed my hands to my face. I could hardly think straight.

"Was it you who tried to kill me?" I said at last, though it was difficult to bring the words out.

"Edmund had a hand in some of the attempts. He bungled them purposely. I didn't really want you dead until I had the map."

"But, Uncle," I said, gripping my hands together, "you nearly succeeded when you shot at me."

"Ah, yes. I admit to making a blunder there, but then I had to deal with Greyson, too, which made things a little difficult."

"You couldn't have shot Greyson! He was your son!"

I almost screamed the words, and my uncle laughed unpleasantly. "That's where you are wrong. He was only my stepson, although he never knew it himself."

He came around until he was facing me. "Nothing was mine, you see, in spite of all I'd done to bring the boy up to the best of my ability. I was to gain nothing from it all." He smiled. "Greyson had Winston, and you, my dear Charlotte, had the Plas; only we must change all that. You must make a will leaving everything to me."

"Won't people think that's rather odd?" I said, trying to speak reasonably.

He shrugged. "Why not? Who else could you leave it to? Everyone else is dead."

"Well, Uncle, you are going to be a lonely old man," I said quickly. "There won't be anyone to enjoy it all with."

"A rich man is never lonely, my dear Charlotte. Haven't you yet learned that much about life?" He moved nearer to me. "Come now, enough talking. Lead the way to your room, and we'll get the map."

Obediently I walked along the corridor, even though I knew the gesture was utterly useless—there was no map that I knew of. When I reached my room, I tried again.

"Uncle, please, I don't know where the map is."

He jabbed me viciously with the gun, and I knew it was useless to argue. I went through the motions of looking inside my cupboard, with Uncle Tom leaning over my shoulder all the while, in case he might miss something.

"Ah, there it is. Very sensible of you, Charlotte."

He drew out a folded paper that crackled as he

opened it. I watched in amazement. I had no idea
where it had come from.

"Good. This is very explicit. Let's go," he said,
and pushed me to the door.

"Go where, Uncle?" I asked in dismay.

He stood looking at me impatiently for a moment.
"Why keep up the pretense, Charlotte? We were both
after the money and precious stones, but you have
lost. Take your defeat in good spirit, that's what I
say! Now over to the chapel—quickly!"

It was cold under the bright stars, and the grass
brushed fingers of dampness across my ankles. It
seemed unreal to be walking through the gardens with
a gun pointing at my back, and Uncle Tom of all
people holding the trigger. And yet there was a feeling
of relief inside me that Greyson hadn't, after all,
tried to kill me, though a lot of good that knowledge
would do me now.

The curved wooden doors stood open, and the interior of the chapel looked eerie and strange in the
dimness. Uncle Tom lifted the lantern high, looking
around suspiciously. Then he indicated that I should
enter first, and reluctantly I obeyed.

It was difficult getting the trap door open, but at
last Uncle Tom was forced to put down the lantern
and the gun and assist me.

I took the slim chance his temporary disadvantage
gave me and thrust back the door suddenly, racing

away down the stone steps and almost pitching head-long in my terror. At the foot of the stairs I tripped over something and to my horror saw that it was the body of William, the coachman. Greyson had been telling me the truth all along; that was becoming increasingly evident.

"You won't get far down there without the map, so come back, and I'll make a deal with you!"

I didn't stop to consider which passage to take; I just rushed into any entrance in my eagerness to be away from Uncle Tom. There would be no deal; just a quick and sudden death. He wanted everything for himself.

Breathless, I stopped, my heart pounding so loudly it seemed as though my uncle must hear it. It was totally dark now, and I felt suffocated by the thick blackness. But there was no point in standing still, waiting to be caught. I had no alternative but to go on into the passage.

Several times I slipped and ended up on my knees, but I forced myself to keep calm; panic would get me nowhere at all.

It seemed I had been walking for hours, but I knew it was in reality only a few minutes since I had entered the passage. It must go somewhere, I reasoned to myself, and if I continued to walk I would find a way out eventually. That is, if Uncle Tom didn't find me first.

I thought my eyes were playing tricks on me, but then when I blinked and looked again I could see plainly that a bobbing light was coming toward me.

I crouched against the wall, wondering in a moment of sheer panic what to do. If I started running in the opposite direction, there was no doubt that my uncle would catch me, or at least get within firing distance. No! the best idea would be to keep perfectly still until I could rush him and hope the surprise attack would catch him off guard.

The light came nearer, and I almost stopped breathing, bracing myself for action.

"Charlotte, where are you?"

I stiffened in sudden shock; the voice calling my name was a woman's! As she drew nearer, I could see the dark dress and the long black hair swinging back from thin shoulders. I pressed myself against the cold wall, unable to move as she came nearer still, holding the swinging lantern high over her hollow face.

She halted only a few feet away from me, and I struggled to stop the scream that rose to my throat. She reached out a bony hand, and my heart stopped beating.

"Charlotte," she said, and gripped my arm.

I wished I could fall senseless so that the terror would be over, but although I closed my eyes and opened them slowly, the horrible apparition was still there.

"Miss Charlotte, are you ill?" I was stunned into stillness. This was no ghostly figure—come to think of it, ghosts needed no lanterns to see the way!

"Wenna?" I asked fearfully, and clasped my fingers over hers.

"Yes, miss, it's me. Come along this way. You'll be all right."

She turned and led the way back down the passage, and with a sigh of relief, I followed her.

"Uncle Tom is a murderer," I said, and my voice echoed strangely down the flat stone wall.

She turned and put her finger to her lips. "Don't let him hear you. He doesn't know I'm still at the Plas. He sent me away, you see."

She didn't give any further explanation, and I kept silent, though there were a hundred questions I wanted to ask. Right now she was my key out of that place, and for the moment that was my main concern.

Presently the passage broadened out into what seemed to be a dead end. Wenna went to the wall and flicked her hand over something; the wall separated, and an entrance opened up before my eyes.

"You just look in there, my dear child. All the money and jewels you could ever want."

I followed her through the door and shivered at the sudden dank coldness that wrapped itself round me like a blanket.

There were two stone vaults dominating the cave-like room. Wenna touched an engraving on one of the lids, and it slid across sideways, with a sort of groaning noise. Inside was jewelry which sparkled and gleamed in the light from the lantern. There were several wooden chests with the lids forced open to reveal exquisite plate and ornaments wrought in silver and gold.

"But this doesn't belong to the Plas, Wenna. Surely it belongs to the families hereabouts?"

She shook her head. "Your mother was killed for it, just as you almost were. I had no proof, you see, so what could I do but help you the only way I knew how?"

There was a lump in my throat as I squeezed Wenna's hand.

"Here are some documents," she said after a moment. "I don't read English, but they were your mother's, so I kept them for you."

Quickly I looked through them; one was a marriage certificate.

"Wenna, look at this! I'm not illegitimate after all! My mother was married, and no doubt Uncle Tom knew it all the time."

Wenna's eyes grew vague. "He tricked me," she said. "I knew there was a wedding, but he said I was mad." Her eyes, too bright in her pale face, met mine. "It was after the death of your mother, you see; the shock was too great for me." She held her hand to her heart as if she could still feel the pain. "I even agreed to give you a drug your uncle left me. He said it would help you sleep. He promised me that was all it was."

"It's all right, Wenna," I said soothingly. "You aren't to blame for anything."

"Very touching indeed!"

We both jumped violently as Uncle Tom appeared in the doorway, brandishing his gun. I was taken completely by surprise. Wenna leaped toward him and pushed him outside, and the door swung gently until it had closed entirely.

I rushed toward it and beat helplessly against it with my fists.

"Wenna, let me out. I can help you!"

There was the sound of a shot, and then for a moment an agonizing silence. A shower of dust fell down from the roof, making me cough. From outside I heard a movement, and then Uncle Tom's voice, muffled by the thickness of the rock.

"Wenna's dead. You might as well open up. You are a prisoner in there, and all the gold and jewels in the world won't do you any good."

I sat still, staring at the lantern, wondering how long the flame would burn.

"All right. I'll leave you for a while, and see how

you feel when you've been in there alone for a few hours."

There was nothing I could do. I didn't know how to open the door, even if I had wanted to.

"Uncle Tom—" I pressed my face against the cold stone—"try to find the lever. It's out there somewhere. Can't you see it on the map?"

But he'd gone. There was no answer except the hollow sound of my own voice bouncing off the rocks.

I looked down at the riches inside the vault. So many people had died because of them, and yet now they were as worthless to me as pieces of glass.

I sat down on a boulder and rested my chin on my hands. Poor Wenna. She had obviously been unbalanced. She hadn't even known what she was doing half the time. She might even have imagined that she was really my mother when she brought me those priceless gifts.

I became aware of a strange rustling sound, and with shaking hands I lifted the lantern high. To my consternation, I saw there was water seeping under the rock door. The tide must be coming in. Greyson had said that the underground passages became flooded when the tide was high.

Quickly I scrambled up onto the vault and watched in horrified fascination as the level of the water rose rapidly. Suddenly I heard the muffled sound of the chapel bell ringing out its warning of a high tide, and I shuddered, wondering who could be ringing the bells. Was it Uncle Tom, glorying in his sick mind because I was trapped?

I screamed as the water lapped over the edge of the vault, and I lifted the lantern high, trying desperately to find another way out.

Towering up from the head of the vault was a cross, and I drew a sharp breath. Could this be the cross I'd seen from my window? I examined it closely. It was just like any other cross, but was it the one on the island? If so, there must be an opening somewhere in the roof, and I must be out in mid-water under the island!

I stood on tiptoe, trying to hold the lantern high, and dug hopefully at the rock with my fingers. Dust showered down on me, but doggedly I continued to dig at the damp hard surface, knowing it was my only hope of escape.

The water was now swirling around my legs, and I glanced down in terror. If I had been standing on the floor instead of on the top of the vault, the water would have been over my head.

The muscles in my legs ached intolerably from the strain of standing on tiptoe, but somehow I kept on trying, and the water continued to rise relentlessly.

At last, sobbing in desperation, I hung onto the cross to rest for a moment. The lantern had almost burned itself out, and in a short while I would be in complete darkness. A numbness seemed to be creeping over me with the advance of the water, and my attempts to probe against the roof became feeble and half-hearted.

"Charlotte!" Was it my imagination, or was there a voice really calling me? "Charlotte, can you hear me?"

Suddenly I was spurred into frenzied activity.

"Greyson, is that you? Oh, Greyson, get me out of here!"

"Charlotte, get a grip on yourself and listen carefully."

I could barely hear what he was saying. There was a buzzing in my ears, and I realized consciousness was slipping away from me.

"There's a spring at the base of the cross. If you press it, it will release the door, and I can get you out. Charlotte, please try, for my sake."

I took a deep breath and plunged beneath the dark icy water. My fingers struggled to find the spring. I kicked around for a few minutes, then rested against the cross. The light had gone out now, and it was totally dark.

I knew I would have to hurry. There wasn't much time left before the water would be over my head. I held onto the stem of the cross so that I wouldn't float away, and carefully felt around the base, thinking that at any moment my lungs would burst. Then my hand encountered a bump in the smooth surface of the cross, and I pressed it with all my strength.

For a moment I thought nothing was going to happen. Then the water began to swirl around me, the cross was rising through a square opening in the rock, and I was being dragged out of the water with it. The mechanism stopped, and then I was in Greyson's arms.

"Charlotte, my poor dear girl!" He held me tightly, and I clung to him in a passion of relief.

"I thought you were dead," I said, my voice rising on a sob. "Uncle Tom told me he'd shot you!"

"He only thought he had," Greyson said bitterly. "I had the sense to roll down the rocks and stay still until I saw Edmund pull you out of the water. I did some probing around after that, and Mrs. Grifiths told me most of the story." He threw his coat around me. "Come on; let's get you to the boat."

"What did Mrs. Grifiths have to do with it?" I asked through teeth that chattered with cold.

Greyson pulled away from the island before answering my question.

"She supplied Father with the poison and other drugs—against her will, of course. You were right when you said someone was there the day we visited her. It was Father. Don't worry; she's told me he's not my real father. And yet I would have trusted him with my life; that's where I made my big mistake."

"You suspected me, didn't you?" I said softly. "Where is Uncle Tom now?"

Greyson jerked his head in the direction of the house. I looked up and saw that all the windows were glowing with light, and there seemed to be a great deal of activity going on.

"I've got plenty of help." Greyson smiled. "Half the town is up there. We caught Father ringing the bell in the chapel. I didn't realize how much strength he had."

"Poor Greyson," I said softly. "But anyway, the townspeople will be well rewarded for their trouble. There's a whole load of priceless jewels and silver and gold down there under the island. Graig Melyn will be a rich town."

"We'll leave them to sort things out," Greyson said with feeling. "As soon as we get to the shore, you are going to change into some dry clothes, and then we are heading straight for Winston."

The boat bumped gently against the shore, and Greyson lifted me out.

"I love you, Charlotte," he said softly. "I didn't realize how much until you were trapped under the island. I felt like digging into the rock with my bare hands."

He cupped my face and kissed me tenderly, and I leaned against him, dizzy with happiness. Arm in arm, we walked up the garden path toward the house.

On the terrace, I stopped for a moment and looked back at the island, almost submerged beneath the sea. The cross stood out sharply against a sky that was beginning to warm with the promise of daybreak, and there were tears in my eyes as I thought of Wenna.

Greyson's arm tightened around me.

"It's all over, my darling," he said softly. "I am taking you home."

Leaning against his strength, I left the darkness and walked into the warmth and light and the certainty of a new day of happiness.